NICK

NICK

ALMA J. YATES

Deseret Book Company
Salt Lake City, Utah

Library of Congress Cataloging-in-Publication Data

Yates, Alma J.
    Nick / Alma J. Yates.
        p.   cm.
    Summary: Aaron, a law student, takes a summer job in a small town
in Utah where he coaches Nadine "Nick" Jerard and meets his long
-absent father.
        ISBN 1-57345-062-6
        [1. Fathers and sons—Fiction. 2. Forgiveness—Fiction.
3. Christian life—Fiction. 4. Mormons—Fiction.] I. Title.
PZ7.Y2125Ni   1995
[Fic]—dc20   95-36488
                                                                    CIP
                                                                    AC

Printed in the United States of America

10   9   8   7   6   5   4   3   2   1

*To my wife, Nicki, whose loving support
and tireless encouragement give me the
determination to reach ever higher.*

Chapter One

Aaron Solinski opened the door of his yellow Honda Civic and prepared to drop into the driver's seat. Suddenly he froze, staring over the gasoline pumps toward the street. In the darkness all he could see was the silhouette of a young woman who was walking on the sidewalk, but he was positive he recognized her. "Hey, Brittany," he called, leaning his forearms on the top of the car door.

She stopped. "Aaron?"

"It *is* you." He laughed, pushing away from the car. He was in his mid-twenties, just under six feet tall, and athletic. "Even in the dark, lugging that armload of books, I could tell it was you."

The young woman crossed the street. "I didn't know you were in Provo, Aaron. What brings you up from the Valley of the Sun? Or doesn't ASU require its law students to study in the spring?" She stood there, smiling warmly, wearing blue denim jeans and an oversized BYU sweatshirt.

"Brittany Cole," Aaron mused, smiling under the fluorescent glow of the gas station lights. "I was just passing through Provo and stopped here for gas. And I bump into you." He looked around. "What are you doing out by yourself at ten-thirty, lugging half the library down the street?"

"Oh, I have a paper due, and, like always, I've put it off too long."

"You don't drive a car anymore?"

Brittany laughed and rested her stack of books on the hood of the Civic. "I wanted the exercise." She smiled and tossed her head. "But I forgot that I was going to have to bring home a few extra books."

When she smiled she showed a mouthful of perfect teeth. They looked especially white against the smooth, tanned skin of her face. Her thick, brown hair was cut short.

"Your hair's different," he said.

"Yeah. Well, you know."

"It looks good."

"Thanks. You look good too."

She studied Aaron's face. His dark eyes teased from a sunburned face. His jaw was a bit square and showed the bluish hue of a heavy beard. Though he wasn't classically good-looking, he had thick, dark hair and a handsomeness that reminded her why she had been so attracted to him.

"I hear you're engaged," Aaron commented.

Brittany held up her left hand and showed him the ring. Aaron nodded and cocked his head.

"What's he like?"

"You'd like him. His name's Cory Slade. He's a business major. He'll graduate this spring and then start on his MBA in the fall."

"Your *dad* will love that."

"It just happened that way. Dad didn't have any input. I'd like you to meet him, but he's out of town this weekend. His grandmother passed away. The funeral's tomorrow."

"I'll have to catch him another time."

Aaron pushed his hands into the pockets of his faded Levi's and looked into Brittany's eyes. They were blue, though they looked dark tonight. She was just as beautiful as Aaron remembered. That beauty had first caught his eye in their modern-dance class, but her exuberance and abundant friendliness had eventually drawn Aaron to her.

"Can I give you a ride home? Or do you have time to get something to eat? I was just going to grab a burger."

She glanced down at her ring.

He held up his hands. "Hey, you're safe with me. You never worried about me before."

"Then I was engaged to you, not someone else."

"Cory doesn't have to worry about me. I'm on my way out of town tonight."

"You're driving back to Arizona *tonight?*"

He shrugged and nodded.

"How are you going to stay awake?"

"Sunflower seeds and determination. I'll catch a few winks along the way. I'm not exactly on spring break, you know."

"I thought everyone at ASU was on spring break from January to the end of May."

"Really funny. Will you let me take you someplace to eat?"

"Are you engaged?"

"Not by a long shot."

"No girls in Tempe?"

"Oh, there are lots of girls. There were lots of girls here. I'm just not your usual guy. You should know that."

Brittany laughed, shaking her head. "Once Dad said he would have loved having you for a son-in-law, but . . . "

"Always that infamous *but.*"

"Dad liked you. He said you were well mannered, talented, intelligent."

"I'll have to have your dad write my resume."

"But," Brittany continued, "Dad said you could be the senior partner in the most prestigious law firm in the country, and it wouldn't be inconceivable for you to wake up one morning and bag it all to open your own two-bit hot dog stand."

"I don't even like hot dogs. Now if it were an ice cream cart or a taco wagon, I'd jump at something like that." He laughed. "All this talk of food is making me hungry. Jump in."

She hesitated. "I still have some studying to do."

"Remember that little place downtown?"

She shook her head and looked down. "Not there."

"But I thought you liked it."

"I did," she answered softly. "Maybe that's why I've never been back. Why don't you just take me home?"

"How about McDonald's?" he asked quickly. "I'm going to faint, I'm so hungry."

Ten minutes later they were sitting in a booth at McDonald's with Brittany's books stacked on the table across the aisle from them.

"You haven't told me what brings you back to Provo."

"My nephew Trent was the lead in his school's fourth-grade play this afternoon. He invited me up."

"What?" She set down her Big Mac and stared across the table. "You drove all that way just to see a school play? What is it, about a twelve-hour drive?"

"Fourteen. But yesterday morning, I was laboring over this legal brief, some ridiculous case about water rights in Podunk, Wyoming. I was bored out of my mind. Trent had called me the night before to tell me about his play. All of a sudden I got this uncontrollable urge to—"

"Open a two-bit hot dog stand," Brittany cut in with a laugh.

Aaron stared at her. He shook his head. "No, I told you that I hate hot dogs. But," he added, "I have this powerful penchant for Davy Crockett plays. Trent was surprised out of his head. His mom told me that if he had won an Oscar, it wouldn't have meant as much as my being there. Now, wasn't that worth the trip?"

"Fourteen hours, one way?"

"But I'm rested up. I could argue before the Supreme Court now. And win! And Trent." He smiled, shaking his head. "Don't you ever miss my impetuous ways?"

"I thought we had agreed that *maddening* was a more accurate description."

"That was your word, not mine."

She opened her mouth to speak but changed her mind and took another bite.

"Where are you living now?" Aaron asked.

She answered with her mouth full. "Presley Manor."

"Presley Manor!" Aaron scoffed. "You didn't."

"Aaron, Presley Manor's no different from any other place."

"Maybe you haven't seen some of the other places."

"I like the view from up there. I would be content to live in a grass hut if I could just keep the view. Of course, it would have to be a pretty good grass hut," she added, laughing. "It would have to have a few amenities. You know, a spiral staircase, maid service, an indoor pool. Just a few of the essentials."

Aaron smiled and shook his head. Brittany could afford the kind of luxury Presley Manor offered. Her father was a well-to-do businessman in Southern California and lived with his family in a huge, rambling, six-bedroom home.

"I didn't think I'd see the day when you would move up on the big hill."

"If you had stayed, maybe I wouldn't have moved. BYU does have a law school, you know."

He smiled, nodding. Actually, BYU had been his first choice, but after he and Brittany had broken off their engagement, he needed to get away, to make the break final. ASU gave him that chance.

"If you had lived at Presley Manor when I knew you, the

old Civic would have developed a complex, parked among the Corvettes and Porsches."

"I liked the Civic. The Civic's quaint."

"Quaint!" Aaron laughed. "Quaint does sound better than beat-up."

He smiled wanly and studied her face for a moment. "I guess it was good that I moved to ASU. If I had stayed, I might not have let Cory come along."

"Perhaps." She swallowed, feeling an emotion that made it difficult to breathe. "I'll always remember the first time we met." She was smiling, but there was a slight catch in her voice. "I really hadn't expected to meet someone like you in a modern-dance class. There were only two other guys in the whole class. And they were just a little, well, you know." She rolled her eyes. "And here you come into the room in your Levi's, T-shirt, and boots. The other two guys kind of fit in, but I kept wondering what had provoked *you* to sign up."

Aaron bowed his head and chuckled, rubbing the back of his neck.

"Then when Sister Wilson started talking about wearing leotards, you jumped up and shouted 'Leotards? You mean those tight stocking pants? Just to do a waltz or the Charleston?'"

"Well, when I saw 'Modern Dance,' I just figured it was a class where I could learn how to do the swing and the waltz and the two-step. How was I to know we'd be flitting around, pretending to be butterflies?"

"After your outburst, I figured you were partly normal. When you dropped the class, I knew you were okay."

"You know, I don't tell very many people about my one and only encounter with modern dance."

Brittany giggled into the back of her hand. "I would like to have seen you at least once in a pair of pink tights."

"Hey, don't rub it in. Let's change the subject. Okay?"

"What are your plans for this summer?" she asked.

"I had an offer to clerk for one of the big law firms in Scottsdale. It's a pretty prestigious place."

"Wonderful."

"But I've decided not to take it."

"What?"

"It's too hot in the Valley during the summer. I can do without the 120-degree heat."

"So where are you going?"

"I'm going to spend the summer in Bear River City. I've just come from there."

"Bear River City!" She stared at him, searching his face for any sign of teasing or mischief. "Why Bear River City?"

"My sister Regina and her kids live there."

"I've got a brother living in Saudia Arabia, but I'm not going to spend the summer there."

"Once you said you liked Bear River."

"But it's just a little dip in the road."

Aaron chewed a couple of fries. "Regina's getting divorced. She's lonely and having a struggle. She needs some company while she and the kids make the adjustment."

"But what will you do?"

"I've got a job working on a road construction crew, driving truck."

"You can't be serious."

Aaron smiled and then began to chuckle. "What's wrong with driving truck?"

"Nothing, if you're illiterate and can't do anything else. But you're finishing your first year of law school. You need to be working in a law office, not out driving a dump truck."

"Hey. I've always *wanted* to drive a dump truck."

"Aaron, you *are* joking, aren't you."

He shook his head. "I start the first week in June,

putting in a highway west of Tremonton. And then there's
another stretch of road we're going to do up in Idaho."

"How long have you had this crazy notion in your
head?"

He shrugged. "I've been thinking about it for a while."

"You just opened a hot dog stand."

Aaron smiled.

"Once you talked of teaching English," she reminded
him. "Do you still think of that?"

Aaron tugged on his ear and looked down at his food.
"Sometimes. You know, late at night, when I'm poring over
a pile of law books, I'll think to myself that I'd love to be out
coaching some track team." He laughed and got a far-off
look in his eyes. "Sometimes I even dream of returning to
Peru and teaching English down there. Ever since my
mission, I've wanted to go back. I just need the right
excuse."

"And if you could teach English down there, you'd go?"

"I'd certainly consider it. I loved Peru. I loved the
people."

"There are people here, too, Aaron. And ways to make a
living other than teaching English."

"You could never have considered marrying an English
teacher-coach or a Peruvian professor, could you? Or a truck
driver?"

"You want to drive truck all your life?"

Aaron shook his head. "Just this summer."

Brittany smiled. "I guess I was never brave enough for
you. I wouldn't make a very good hot dog matron." She
became serious. "But sometimes I wish I were more like
you."

"Now, Miss Brittany," Aaron drawled, "don't you go
gettin' sentimental on me."

She smiled sadly. "Good luck, Aaron. I hope you love

driving truck. Maybe you'll meet some winsome farm girl and fall in love." She reached out and touched the back of his hand with the tips of her fingers. "I've always been glad that we were able to walk away from each other and still be friends. You'll come to my reception, won't you?" She smiled. "If you'll drive fourteen hours to see a Davy Crockett play, surely you can make it to my reception."

Aaron stared at her. His smile faded. "Brittany, it's taken me about a year. I don't think about us very much anymore. Of course, tonight probably sets me back a month or so." He shrugged. "But I'm glad I spotted you." He swallowed and looked away. "But I'd better let you do the reception by yourself. I'll take your word for it that Cory's a great guy."

He stood up. "I'd better get you home and me on the road."

Brittany looked up at him without moving. "I'll walk."

"With all those books? The old Civic won't even mind rubbing fenders with the Porsches and the BMWs."

She shook her head. "I'd like the walk. Besides, it's better that way."

Aaron smiled and nodded his head. Turning, he stepped into the night without looking back.

Chapter Two

A warm, late-afternoon sun blazed golden across the slow, winding Bear River. Just east of the river two hay rigs—a tractor pulling a flat-bed trailer and a pickup truck pulling a wagon—were working from opposite corners of an alfalfa field. The pickup had finished loading and was in the lead. The tractor-trailer rig was racing to pick up half a dozen bales still lying in the field.

Halfway across the field the pickup truck hit a small irrigation dike and the load of hay bales shuddered and tilted. "Take it easy, Nick, or you'll throw us right into the river!"

The truck skidded to a stop, and the three men on top groped frantically for a handhold to steady themselves. "I thought you wanted to win," the driver complained shrilly.

"We'd like to make it to the barn in one piece. You've been driving like a maniac! We didn't ask for a carnival ride."

"Maybe I'll give you something you didn't ask for. But something you deserve." Nick ground the gears and gunned the engine, and the three on top dropped to their hands and knees and eventually to their bellies. They hung on desperately as the truck lurched hazardously across the field, bouncing over dikes, bumps, and ditches and careening wildly through a gate onto the narrow county road. Swinging onto the road, the truck swerved to the far side and then cut back sharply to the near side. The load teetered and swayed, and five bales toppled from the wagon. Again gears growled and groaned, and the rig raced toward a huge barn set in an orderly arrangement of sheds, corrals, and a red brick farmhouse shaded by tall cottonwood trees.

As the truck rolled into the yard, it slowed momentarily and then cut sharply at the corner of the barn. Four more bales toppled from the wagon, and the rig came to an abrupt halt. The load trembled and another half dozen bales tumbled from the truck to the ground in an explosion of dust and flying hay leaves. The truck door swung open and out stepped a nineteen-year-old woman.

She was just under five-feet-nine with her scuffed and battered boots on, but even though she was dressed more like a cowboy than a young lady, the jeans, the flannel shirt with the rolled-up sleeves, and the boots didn't disguise her beauty. She glared up defiantly at her three brothers. Her hands were on her hips, and her brown eyes flashed angrily. "Don't tell me how to drive, Jared Jerard. You've been griping about my driving for seven years, and I drive better than all of you."

The two younger brothers, identical twins, staggered unsteadily to their feet, glancing first at their older brother and then at their fuming sister.

A moment later the tractor-trailer rig pulled into the yard with three more brothers. Two were in their twenties; the other, a few months past eighteen. From the seat of the tractor, the oldest of the six brothers glanced up at the three standing atop the jumbled first load of hay and remarked, "The idea is to put the hay in the barn, not scatter it all over the county."

"Just shut up, Jeremiah," Jared growled.

Jeremiah hopped down from the tractor and pulled his leather gloves from his back pocket. "And you guys said you could outdo an old married man, a fat buck just off his mission, and a kid that just graduated from high school." He chuckled, shaking his head.

Jeremiah turned to Nick. "If you're not working for those three any more, do you think you could move that rig and back ours into the barn where we can unload it?"

Nick ran her fingers through her blonde, wind-blown hair. She climbed into the truck and moved the first hay rig and then mounted the tractor, and with the skill that seven years of experience and fraternal coaching had given her, she maneuvered the tractor and trailer neatly through the open barn doors and eased it up against the hay already stacked inside.

"Nobody drives a rig like Nick," Jeremiah laughed as he, Joshua, and Jacob climbed up on the trailer to unload it.

"You can cut the flattery, Jeremiah," she snapped.

Jeremiah held up his hands. "I won't say another word. We could use a big jug of ice water, though."

Nick glanced at her other three brothers. Her full lips twisted into a frown. Then smiling back at Jeremiah, Jacob, and Joshua she answered pleasantly, "I'd love to. But," she quickly added, "*those* three can get their own drinks." She turned and headed for the house.

"Jared, you've got to treat her delicately," Jeremiah grunted, jerking up on a bale and tossing it up to Jacob on the hay stack.

"I know how to treat Nick."

"I guess that's why half your load's still in the field."

A battered '57 Chevy pickup truck pulled up to the side of the house just as Nick came out the back door carrying a large jug of water. The Chevy's driver stepped out and greeted her with a nod. "Hi. I'm looking for Jared Jerard. Is this his place?"

"He thinks so. But he just lives here like the rest of us."

The man pushed his hands into his back pockets.

Without appearing to stare, he studied Nick a moment, noting the smooth, tanned complexion and the dark eyes. "I'm Aaron Solinski," he said. "Is Jared around?"

Nick nodded toward the barn. "I'll take you over." They walked a few paces. "So you're Aaron. You're not what I expected."

"Oh?"

She smiled. "I was expecting you to be wearing a beard, smoking, and chewing." She laughed. "I'm Nick, Jared's sister." She held out her hand.

Aaron stopped and stared. "Jared's kid sister?" Nick nodded. Aaron's smile quickly evolved into a chuckle. He shook Nick's extended hand. "When Jared said he had a little sister named Nick, I pictured a runny-nosed kid in bib overalls, pigtails, and freckles, someone just about old enough to always be in the way."

"That figures," Nick bristled.

"Jared says you work for J. T. Overson Construction." Nick nodded. "I'll have to make it a point to stop by the office occasionally."

"About the only truck drivers who show up in J.T.'s office are the ones who are there to pick up their pink slips."

"Maybe I'll just wave as I drive past, then."

She smiled and looked away. "Jared, someone here to see you."

Jared straightened up. He smiled and waved. "Aaron! What brings you out this way?"

"You left your lunchbox on the hood of your truck. I brought it out to you. When you said your place was just across the river, I didn't realize I'd have to swim across. I followed the road you told me about, but when I got to the end of it, the only place there was to go was right into the river."

"I must have forgotten to tell you about the left turn.

You go down *that* road a mile to the bridge and then double back on the other side."

"Looks like you lost part of your load down the road. Somebody doesn't know how to stack."

Nick smiled and looked up at Jared.

"I see you got your sister's old Chevy running," Jared said, ignoring Nick.

"All it needed was a little tuning and cleaning. It doesn't look like much, but with a good paint job, Regina will have a hot little truck. If you'll drive," he said, turning to Nick, "I'll go back and pick up those bales."

"You ever buck bales?" Jared asked.

"I figure I can get them to the barn. That's better than you farmboys have done."

"I don't like anybody telling me how to drive," Nick remarked.

Aaron put up his hands. "You drive any way you want."

Nick smiled. "You've got yourself a driver."

"Let me introduce you to the clan," Jared said. He nodded toward Jeremiah. "That's my big brother Jeremiah. He owns a place down the road. He also teaches math at the high school during the winter. But he comes home when it's haying season. The one in the ugly hat is my younger brother Joshua. He just got off a mission in Guatemala." Joshua nodded a greeting and grinned. "The other one over there is Jacob. He graduated from high school a week or so back. And these two here," he said, pointing to the twins, "are Joseph and James. They've got a year left in high school. But they figure they know all there is to know right now."

"I take it your folks were a bit partial to the scriptures," Aaron remarked to Nick as they both climbed into his truck and headed back for the rest of the hay.

Nick laughed. "Our dad, Jacob Jerard, loved the

scriptures. He dreamed of having twelve sons. And a daughter. Just like Jacob in the Bible. He planned to name the first six sons from the Bible and the next six from the Book of Mormon." She shrugged. "He got his six biblical sons and me, and then he was thrown from a horse and killed."

"I don't remember a Nick in the Bible or in the Book of Mormon."

Nick pulled up to the first few bales strewn along the road. "Nick isn't my real name," she explained. "Dad liked names that started with J. There aren't many female biblical names that start with J. Jezebel in the Bible didn't have the reputation that Dad wanted to perpetuate, so he was going to name me Esther Ruth. Then Mom asserted her maternal prerogative and insisted I be named Nadine, after a sister of hers. When I was little, my brothers thought I was spoiled, so they called me Picki-Nicki. That changed to Nicki." She shrugged. "Eventually, Nicki became Nick."

"What's it like to be the only girl in a family of boys?"

She smiled. "I get along with them most of the time." She looked over at him. "But it's not easy living with six guys who all think they're your dad." She sighed and laughed. "Don't get me wrong." She took a deep breath as Aaron bucked the last bale into the back of the truck. "I love them, but they don't understand me any more. I'm not still a little, freckle-faced girl in pigtails and bib overalls. I spent the last year at USU being independent and managing just fine. Being home the last few days has been a bit of an adjustment for all of us."

Aaron wiped his brow with the back of his hand and asked, "Your mother didn't ever remarry?"

Nick shook her head as she turned the truck around and headed for the barn. "She had just turned thirty-one when Dad was killed. She's been a widow ever since. A few of the neighbors tried to get her to sell the farm, but they were more interested in helping themselves than in helping Mom. Mom wouldn't sell. She kept the farm, went back to school, and finished a degree in elementary education. She's taught school and managed the farm ever since. And raised us kids. When the boys were old enough, they took over the farm. They like people to think they're the boss now." She shook her head. "But Mom still calls the shots. As tough as they think they are, not one of them would dare go against Mom."

The six brothers were just finishing unloading when Nick and Aaron drove up. A pretty woman in her middle fifties was standing by the barn door holding a plastic pitcher of colored punch. Nick backed the truck into the barn and hopped out. "Do you think you can take it from here?" she called to her brothers. Turning to the woman holding the drink, she said, "Mom, this is Aaron Solinski. Aaron, this is Ruth Jerard, the *real* boss on this place." She spoke with a smile and a quiet sense of pride.

Mrs. Jerard held out her hand in greeting. Aaron felt immediately the firm grip. Mrs. Jerard was shorter than Nick and still trim. Her short, black hair had a few streaks of gray. She wasn't as fine-featured as Nick, but there was a strong resemblance between the older woman and her daughter, mainly in their eyes and generous smiles. "Have a drink, Aaron. Thanks for helping out."

"Oh, I didn't do much," Aaron protested. "I just dropped off Jared's lunchbox." He looked around. "You've got a nice place here, Mrs. Jerard."

She smiled. "It gives the boys plenty to do."

"Well, I've got to get going," Nick announced.

"Where you off to?" Jeremiah called after her.

"Kip Percy's picking me up in less than an hour."

"Kip Percy?" Jared groaned.

Nick stiffened. "For your information, Jared, Kip and I

are friends. We have been for years. Two years ago you complained about Kip because he wasn't a returned missionary.
Now he's back from his mission."

"Kip could go on a dozen missions, and it wouldn't help
him," Jared came back.

"Jared," Mrs. Jerard cautioned with a smile, "when
you're Nadine's mom or dad, you can give a little more
counsel. And she'll probably be a little more receptive
toward it then. But for the time being . . . " She left the sentence unfinished.

"Richard Robbins is going to be back from his mission
at the end of the summer," Jeremiah injected. "I thought
you were waiting for him, Nick."

"I'm not *waiting* for anybody," Nick answered with an
edge to her voice. "You guys are the ones waiting for
Richard."

"You've been writing him," Jacob pointed out.

"That doesn't mean I have to lock myself into a musty
room and pine away. Richard is a friend, just like Kip."

Aaron cleared his throat. "Hey, Jared," he announced,
waving, "I'll pick you up tomorrow morning. Nice meeting
you, Mrs. Jerard. I'll let you referee this round." He started
for his truck, not wanting to get caught in the middle of a
feud.

"All Kip Percy cares about is finding a pretty face to dec-
orate that fancy red Corvette his dad bought him for going
on his mission," Jared continued to press as Aaron pulled
out of the barn and drove off.

"You don't have any right to judge Kip Percy," Nick
flared.

"That's enough, boys," Mrs. Jerard cut in, putting her
arm around Nick and pulling her toward the house. "Nadine
isn't planning her wedding just yet," she called over her

shoulder, "so she won't need your fatherly advice for a while longer."

As the brothers slapped hay leaves from their clothes, James shrugged and commented, "We could waylay him at the bridge. Stop him and run him back to town."

"What we need to do," Jared said pensively, "is find someone for Nick until Richard gets home. I don't care what she says; she *is* waiting for Richard. She just doesn't like to admit it."

"You start matchmaking for your sister," Jeremiah warned, "and you're going to be in more trouble than you were on top of that load of hay."

Although it was still light by the time Aaron drove up to his sister's place in Bear River City, the sun had dropped from sight and the evening was rapidly evolving into night. He stepped from the truck and glanced about his sister's yard, which was enclosed by a low chain-link fence. Some petunias were starting to fill in a neat bed just inside the fence and rose bushes thrived along the front of the house. The modest frame home was painted an inviting yellow with white shutters at the windows and wind chimes hanging about the covered porch.

Aaron sauntered up the walk, pushed open the front door, and inhaled deeply. He smelled his supper waiting for him in the kitchen.

"I was beginning to wonder if you were going to make it," Regina called to him from the kitchen sink as he spotted his place at the kitchen table. "The kids and I ate. Wash up and I'll have yours warm."

Aaron washed and returned to the kitchen. He watched Regina work. She was young, just three years older than he. She had always been pretty. With her short, brown hair and bluish gray eyes that smiled out of a round, girlish face, she looked more like a teenager than the twenty-nine-year-old mother of three that she was.

She padded to the table in bare feet, wearing faded jeans and an untucked man's dress shirt. She set a bowl of steaming stew on the table in front of Aaron. He was glad to see her looking happy. A month or so earlier, as the divorce battle had intensified and the two lawyers haggled, she had been morose and racked with uncertainty as she wondered if, in spite of Brandon's infidelity, she should give him one more chance. Her face had been pinched with worry. Now the final details of the divorce settlement were falling into place. She had a good job as a secretary in a real estate office in Brigham City, and she was feeling more confident that she could make it on her own. She still had her bad days, but it was more common to see the old sparkle in her eyes and a smile on her lips.

"Now that you've almost finished your first week," Regina called over her shoulder, "do you think you'll survive a whole summer here?"

Aaron stuffed a half slice of bread into his mouth and chewed and talked at the same time. "It's nice to sit in a bouncy old dump truck and just think. About anything. I don't have to worry about the next legal brief or how I'm going to wade through two dozen law cases." He grinned. "I love it."

"You haven't spent a weekend here yet."

Aaron shrugged and reached for another piece of bread. "My weekends weren't all that interesting in Tempe."

"Do you still think of Brittany Cole?"

"I saw her a month ago. When I came up for Trent's play. I was stopped for gas in Provo and spotted her. She's engaged."

"Oh. I was hoping something might still work out

between you two." Aaron shook his head, staring down at his stew.

"You haven't forgotten her, have you?" Regina said.

Aaron thought for a long time. Slowly he shook his head. "No, Regina, I haven't forgotten her."

"Has she forgotten you?"

"Let's just say she's better off with the other guy."

"How can you be so sure?"

"From the time I first met her, something kept telling me that things wouldn't work out. I think Brittany felt it too. There were little hints along the way. The fact that we both decided to break things off didn't have anything to do with our not liking each other. She needs to be the wife of some businessman, someone who can slip right into the Coles' establishment. Her dad had me pegged pretty well. He fig-ured I'd run off and open a hot dog stand someplace."

"And Brittany wouldn't have gone with you?"

"Not a chance."

"Girls who are willing to run off and open a hot dog stand are hard to come by." Regina laughed. "Maybe you ought to plan on being a really good lawyer. Women like a little romance, but they *need* security." She paused. "I do appreciate you for coming," Regina said quietly. "This has been a tough time for me and the kids." She swallowed. "Even now I wonder if Brandon and . . . "

"Regina!"

Regina sat across the table from her brother and fumbled with her hands. "I still love him, Aaron."

Aaron set his spoon down and looked over at his sister. "I thought you had come to grips with that, Regina. He was unfaithful to you. Remember?"

She smiled sadly and leaned forward to set her folded arms on the table. "I'm not saying I could ever go back to him or let him come back to me. But I'll never love anyone like I loved Brandon. Never."

"Regina, he's bad news."

"I remember when you thought he was the greatest guy in the world, Aaron. For you, there was nobody like Brandon Downs."

"That's all changed. Only a scumbag does what he did." He jabbed his spoon in her direction. "I'm telling you right now, if he shows up around here, I'm going to break his head. So help me, I will, Regina. He's not going to mess you up anymore."

"He called this afternoon."

"You didn't talk to him, did you?"

"He wants to see the kids on Saturday. He said he'd drop by to pick them up."

"You don't have to let him," Aaron snapped. "The judge hasn't given him any visitation rights. Let him wait till the divorce is final."

"My lawyer says I have a better chance of maintaining custody if I can show that I've tried to work with Brandon. If Brandon can show that I've been keeping the kids away from him, then that goes against me."

"All right!" Aaron declared emphatically. "But he doesn't have to come here to get the kids. He's just coming to see you. Ever since that other girl dropped him, he's been getting ready to make his move."

"Someone told me he left *her*."

"As far as I'm concerned, it doesn't make much difference. He'll come with his sorrowful, puppy-eyed look and want you to take him back. He'll give you a hundred promises. And none of them any good."

"He's been good about the divorce. At least recently. He could have caused a lot more trouble than he has."

"That's because you could have taken him to the cleaners. He knows that."

She heaved a sigh. "Aaron, I'm not going back to him."

"And he's not coming here. I'll drive the kids in to his place Saturday. And I'll pick them up when he's done with them. If it's the kids he wants to see, he'll see them. But wipe him out of your mind, Regina. He's a dead-end street. I don't see what you see in the guy."

"I lived with him for twelve years." She put her chin in her hand and stared down at the tabletop. "I started dating Brandon when we were both fourteen—two years after Mom and Dad broke up."

"And as far as I'm concerned, AJ's at least partially to blame for you and Brandon."

"Oh, Aaron, you can't blame my problems on Daddy."

"Regina, if AJ hadn't left Mom when he did, a lot of things would have been different for all of us. For one thing, you probably wouldn't have charged off and married Brandon while you were still a kid."

Remembering, Regina smiled ruefully. "We were seventeen. Everyone said we'd never make it." She shook her head. "But we were determined. Oh, Aaron, we tried hard. Those were such tough years, living on almost nothing while we both finished high school, and then he went to college. We didn't have anything but each other. But they were good years."

"Before he started running around."

She ignored the remark. "How he ever finished his degree in accounting while he worked full-time and tried to raise a family too, I'll never know. We were active in the Church. He got his job as a CPA. Everything was almost perfect." She suddenly became solemn. "And then—" She stopped herself and blinked back the mist forming in her eyes.

"I'll take him the kids," Aaron said quietly, staring down thoughtfully into his bowl of stew.

Regina was silent while Aaron finished eating. Pushing away from the table, he carried his dishes to the sink and began rinsing them off. "What do you know about Nick Jerard?" Aaron asked suddenly.

Regina awakened from her silent pondering. She studied her brother. "Where did you run in to Nick?"

"I work with Jared."

"I didn't know that."

"His car is in the garage for the next few days, so I'm giving him a ride to work. I went out to his place this afternoon to take him his lunchbox."

"Nick's a cutie. And lots of fun," Regina said, smiling. "I taught her when she was a Laurel. She can be feisty around her brothers, but she's very warm and friendly." Regina's eyes narrowed as Aaron turned from the sink and began drying his hands on a paper towel. "You don't have your eye on Nick Jerard, do you?"

Aaron tossed the paper towel into a garbage container under the sink. "I hauled hay with her today. In Bear River City, that probably means we're almost engaged." He winked and laughed.

"You hauled hay with her?"

"We made a pretty good team. What else do you know about her?"

"She's no Brittany Cole."

Aaron grinned. "I gathered that from her boots and jeans and the hayseeds in her hair."

"I don't mean that she's a country bumpkin," Regina said. "She's very intelligent and talented. I like Nick. You won't find a better girl."

"The way she stood up to her brothers, she reminded me

of a female John Wayne," Aaron joked. "Without the belly and the swagger, of course."

"Well, your male perception is obviously warped. And if you so much as give her a second look, I hope she gives you a good, hard uppercut to the chin."

"Now that *would* scare me. Maybe I'll have to ask her out and see if I can get an up-close glimpse of her talents, abilities, and intelligence. Is she the kind of girl who would dash off into the wilderness and build a two-bit hot dog stand on nothing more than her impetuous husband's whim?"

"She wouldn't dash off with you anyplace," Regina kidded. "She probably wouldn't give you the time of day. I don't think that Nick is the type to be easily flattered by guys who are impressed by themselves. Even ones in law school."

"Don't worry," Aaron laughed. "She's too young for me. I was just asking what you knew about her."

Chapter Three

"I'm glad I won't be doing this all my life," Jared groaned to Aaron as he stretched and reached for another sandwich while lying in the shade of his parked dump truck.

Aaron grinned. "Me, I needed to get out of the library, see a little light, breathe a little air, even if it does have J. T. Overson Construction sand and gravel in it." He laughed and pushed the last quarter of sandwich into his mouth. "Did you get your sister straightened out last night?"

"That's a full-time job. Do you have sisters besides Regina?"

"Two of them. But I don't try to run their lives. They manage without help from me."

"They must not be like Nick. I'll be glad when she marries Richard Robbins."

"She didn't sound all that smitten by this Richard Robbins."

"The first date she ever had was with Richard."

"Maybe one was enough for her."

"She's written to him his whole mission. He's right for her."

"You don't figure she's smart enough to decide that?" Aaron pushed himself to his feet. "From what I gathered yesterday," Aaron laughed, "she's probably got more brain power than all six of her brothers put together."

After work, as Aaron and Jared climbed into the Civic

and headed for home, Jared said, "I've been thinking this afternoon. You're not dating anybody, are you?"

Aaron shook his head. "I was engaged about a year ago. But that's over now. I haven't been brave enough to try again."

"What happened?"

Aaron explained briefly.

"You're the perfect guy for Nick," Jared said.

Aaron glanced over at Jared. "Why am I the perfect guy for Nick?" he asked.

Jared grinned at Aaron. "Let me tell you what I'm thinking."

"Jared, I can already tell your brain's baked."

"Hear me out." Aaron studied Jared's grinning, teasing face. "You ask Nick out."

"You know, Jerard, I had you pegged for a fairly intelligent guy, but when you start looking out for your kid sister, you lose touch with reality. She doesn't need you to hold her hand any more. She's grown up, in case you haven't noticed."

"Look, Aaron, I'm serious." He struggled to keep the grin off his face.

"That's what has me worried."

"It's perfect. It will give you something to do during the summer. You know, keep your mind off of this Brittany Cole."

"My mind isn't on Brittany Cole. She's getting married at the end of the summer."

Jared ignored him. "And Nick can stay occupied until Richard shows up. Then you go back to Arizona and find another Brittany Cole."

"I'm not looking for another Brittany Cole. If I were, I would have stayed with the first one." Aaron continued to laugh and shake his head. "Besides, do you know how old I am?"

Jared studied Aaron a moment and then shrugged. "Twenty-four?"

"Would you believe twenty-six? Nick was in elementary school when I left on my mission. To her, I'm an old man."

"Nick needs a fatherly figure."

"To date? Or do you think she needs someone to baby-sit her?"

"It would be just for the summer."

"Suppose at the end of the summer," Aaron grinned, "I decide that I don't *want* Richard to take over?"

"Oh, you're too old, too sophisticated for Nick. She's not your type. Take her to the movie tonight. I'll pay."

Smiling and staring down the road, Aaron shook his head. "Jerard, you are definitely a couple of bubbles off plumb. Why the panic over your little sister?"

Jared took in a deep breath. Leaning back in his seat, he exhaled and dug his fingers into his dusty brown hair. "I was three when Nick was born. Everybody thought we were going to have another boy. I just knew we were going to have a girl. For some reason I thought she was *my* sister. From the time she was just a baby, I looked after her. She was only two when Dad was killed. When I went off to school that first fall after Dad's death, she clung to me and wasn't going to let me go. We've always talked and gone places together. When she's had a problem, I've been the one she's come to. When I went on my mission, she became a little more independent. But I still worry about her."

"Jared, she grew up on you. Cut her loose, big brother. She's not going to get lost."

That evening Regina and her kids went to a birthday party at a neighbor's place. Aaron was more in the mood for

a burger and fries than the tuna casserole his sister had waiting for him, so he headed for Tremonton, looking for a place
to eat. For a while he drove up and down the quiet streets,
looking the town over while the cool evening air blew in
through his open car windows.

Tremonton had a population of about ten thousand.
Many of the streets were lined with trees. The yards were
green, well-trimmed, and the town showed evidence of a
quiet pride. It was a far cry from the hectic rush of the
Phoenix area.

With the sun sinking behind the grayish blue hills to the
west, Aaron parked the Civic and started walking down
Main Street. He passed Jeppesen Gym and Fitness Center
and glanced through the plate glass windows at the half
dozen guys sweating and straining as they pumped iron.
Farther on was the Western Trail Dining Room Cafe, a corner eating place with a neon sign that proclaimed:
"Authentic Mexican Food Friday Nights." Aaron was
tempted to slip in, find a quiet booth, and test their authentic fare. He decided instead to continue down the street,
past Coast to Coast Hardware Store, the bank, the Pizza
Company Arcade, Genellies Pizza Parlor, and the other
businesses lining Main Street. At Christensen's Family
Department Store, which was closed, he looked in the window at a poster advertising the Hyrum Rodeo Queen con-
test. He wondered if Nick would be interested.

It was just before nine o'clock when he stopped at
Mack's Family Diner and sauntered in. The dining area was
clean, furnished with white tables and bright yellow vinyl
benches and black chairs. The colors jumped out at him.
There were a half dozen teens inside, a couple playing the
video games in the corner and the others eating and talking
at a table in the center of the room.

Aaron stepped to the counter, ordered a double

hamburger and fries, and then sat down at an empty table with his back to the counter and the door. Waiting for his order, he leaned his elbows on the table and stared out the window as night engulfed the town in darkness. He became vaguely aware of several people entering. At first he didn't allow their voices to disturb his thoughts, but gradually he sensed a confrontation brewing.

"She's coming with me. I brought her in."

"You picked her up."

"Would you two stop it, please," a girl's voice demanded.

"Just back off, Percy, before you get your tail in a crack and can't pull it out."

"You worry about your own tail."

"Stop it, both of you."

"If you want to step outside, we can settle the whole thing."

"Theresa and I will find our own way home. If you two want to butt heads, don't do it over us."

"Come on, Percy, you afraid to step outside?"

Aaron rolled a salt shaker between the palms of his hands, trying to ignore the conversation. Finally his curiosity prompted him to turn. Nick Jerard, with another girl, stood at the counter while two guys faced each other to their right.

"Come on, Percy. I'm calling you out. Or are you scared?" The guy doing most of the talking was wearing blue denim Wrangler jeans, a tight-fitting T-shirt, and cowboy boots. He was also wearing a large belt buckle and a black cowboy hat.

"Don't push your luck, Macey," Percy retorted.

Aaron looked over Kip Percy, who was dressed in faded but well-pressed denim jeans, a knit golf shirt, and a pair of basketball shoes.

Suddenly Macey reached out and took Nick's hand and

pulled her his way. She resisted, jerking her hand out of his grasp. Kip Percy moved forward and pushed Macey backward. Immediately the two were in each other's faces, their jaws locked, their eyes glowering menacingly.

"Grow up!" Nick ordered.

Aaron got to his feet and stepped to the counter, sliding between the two combatants. "Hello," he greeted, smiling at Nick. "You two looking for a ride home?" Nick didn't immediately recognize him.

"Aaron Solinski. We hauled hay yesterday."

Nick smiled, relieved. "Yes, we *do* need a ride. Let's go, Theresa."

"Hey," Macey called out as Aaron and the two young women made their way to the front door. "What's the idea?" He pushed past Kip Percy and approached Aaron. Aaron turned and stood in the doorway as the girls walked out ahead of him. "I'm a friend of the family. I'll get them home while you two finish your discussion." He smiled and patted Macey on the shoulder. Macey shook his hand off. Aaron turned and followed Nick and Theresa outside.

"It's the old, yellow Civic down the street a ways." Aaron laughed. "I promised you a ride home. Not an evening of luxury."

Neither girl spoke as they hurried down the street, pulled open the car door, and climbed in, Theresa in the back and Nick in the front.

"Do you make it a habit of pushing your nose into somebody else's business?" Macey demanded as Aaron stepped off the curb next to his car.

Aaron smiled. "Are you the only one qualified to do that?"

"Don't get smart," Macey warned huskily, blocking Aaron's way.

"You're in the way, Cowboy."

"In a minute I'm going to be right in your face."

"You already are." Aaron chuckled, but there was no humor in his laugh.

Macey reached out and grabbed Aaron's arm just above the elbow. For a moment Aaron looked down at it and then he stared Macey in the eyes, no longer smiling. "Take it off, cowboy." He gave his arm a sudden twisting jerk that tore it free from Macey's grip, and then he planted both his hands in Macey's chest and shoved with one quick movement. Macey flew backward, stumbling first over the curb and then banging into a light pole before he tumbled to the pavement on the seat of his pants. At the same time, Aaron climbed into the Civic, started the engine, and pulled away from the curb as Macey was scrambling to his feet in an embarrassed rage.

For the first several minutes no one in the car spoke. Finally Aaron sucked in a breath of night air pouring in through the open window and commented, "I don't know about you two, but I'm still hungry. And I don't think they're going to save my order back there at the Greasy Spoon or whatever that place was called."

"We'll pay for it," Nick offered.

"I'm not worried about the money. But my stomach's still growling."

"You could stop at the Crossroads. It's out of town, but it's on our way home."

"Is the food good?"

Nick nodded.

Nothing more was said until they pulled in at the Crossroads, a truck stop. Aaron found a parking spot and opened his door. Nick started to open hers. "I'll catch the door," Aaron offered.

"Growing up with six brothers, I learned to open my own doors."

Aaron touched Nick's arm and smiled. "I might be old-fashioned, but when a lady rides in my car, I open the door."

Nick closed the door and shrugged. "All right, we'll play by your rules." While Aaron was coming around the car, the two young women exchanged smiles.

"What are you ordering?" Aaron asked as he picked up a menu inside the Crossroads Restaurant.

Nick and Theresa looked at each other and laughed. "We'd better have water. We pooled our money back in town for a hamburger and fries. We left our order on the counter, too." They both giggled.

"The country girls come to town," Aaron mused. "How about if I buy?"

"We can't let you do that."

"Humor me tonight."

Nick laughed. She glanced over at Theresa and then looked across the table at Aaron. "In all the excitement, I didn't even introduce you to Theresa. Aaron, this is my best friend, Theresa Porter. She lives down the road from us. We've been friends for years. This last year we roomed together at USU."

Aaron nodded at Theresa. She blushed slightly and glanced down at the table. Aaron noticed that she was pretty, with soft brown eyes and a sprinkling of light freckles across her nose and cheeks. When she smiled, a single dimple formed in her left cheek, and her sandy brown hair was cut short.

"So, what brings two girls like you into town on a night like this?" Aaron asked after the waitress had taken their orders.

Nick and Theresa looked at each other and laughed. Nick put her hands flat on the table and answered. "We were both in the mood for a movie. Theresa was going to drive but then she found out her mom needed the car, so I suggested we hitchhike."

"Hitchhike!"

"We used to do it all the time. We'd always get a ride. Kip Percy picked us up. He was one of the guys back at—"

"I remember him."

"Anyway, he picked us up and dropped us at the movie. He had something else to do but was going to drop by later to give us a ride home. Well, Todd Macey—he's the other guy—was at the movie, too, and he gave us a ride to the cafe and—."

"And then you had two guys who didn't want to share."

Nick nodded. "We should have just hitchhiked home."

"You shouldn't have hitchhiked at all."

"We always get a ride with someone we know. Or someone who looks safe. Don't start worrying."

"Who's Todd Macey?"

"We went to school with him. He's a rodeo nut, a real good bull rider. But he's a hothead, as you probably noticed." Aaron nodded. Nick grimaced. "There's something else you ought to know."

"What's that?"

"You didn't make a very good first impression on Todd. He'll probably be looking for you. He's a fighter. A good one."

It was after ten-thirty when the three finally left the Crossroads and headed for Bear River City. Aaron dropped Theresa off and then started for Nick's place. As they approached the Bear River, a big, yellow, full moon was creeping up over the mountains to the east.

"Hey!" Nick called out excitedly. "Stop down on the bridge. Let's watch the moon rise. When it comes up over the mountains like this, it shines across the river and it's absolutely gorgeous. You'll love it from the bridge."

The road wound down into the river bottom and then came to an old metal bridge that spanned the river. Aaron pulled the Civic to the side of the road and the two of them walked from there to the middle of the bridge.

The night air was cool and fresh, and a multitude of chirping crickets and croaking frogs were creating a late-night symphony. The sluggish, murky waters of the Bear River moved silently below them. To the east and a half mile away, the river turned at an almost ninety-degree angle, but for that half mile the placid river became a mirror. The shimmering reflection of the moon was splashed all over the water, creating a scintillating swatch of light.

"What do you think?" Nick asked.

"I didn't think you were the type to get sentimental about a full moon on the river."

Nick laughed. "Why's that?"

"You come across as too . . . too tough."

"That's just around my six brothers. Actually," she added, "I've got a sentimental side. Most people think I'm pretty feminine. Even old-fashioned. My brothers don't know it, though."

Nick leaned forward against the bridge railing and stared out across the river. They were quiet for a moment, blending into the night.

"My brothers are overprotective." Nick turned and rested her back against the bridge. She looked over at him. "In fact, you shouldn't be worrying about Todd Macey. You ought to be worrying about my six brothers. They would have a fit if they knew we were together here on the bridge getting sentimental over a full moon."

Aaron straightened up. "Then I'd better get you home before the search party arrives. Or the lynch mob."

"Oh, you're probably safe, being a friend of Jared's."

"So, I'm no threat?"

She studied him in the darkness. "I think I can trust you."

"But can Richard Roberts?" Aaron asked playfully.

"It's Richard *Robbins*," she sighed. "And Richard isn't worried about me at all right now. Which is the way it should be."

Aaron glanced over at her. She had turned again to look at the moon's reflection, and he could see her silhouette as she gazed out across the river. "So Richard doesn't impress you as much as he does your brothers?"

"We've dated off and on. He *is* a neat guy. He wants to be a doctor. He has his whole life planned out, wrapped up in a neat, trim package." She shrugged. "I'm not sure I want to . . . " She laughed softly. "Maybe I prefer a little more uncertainty in my life. At least right now."

Aaron took Nick's arm and said, "I think I hear the bloodhounds." Slowly they strolled back to the car and headed home.

Chapter Four

Aaron heard the clatter of plates and pans and smelled the fresh aroma of bacon and biscuits before he ever opened his eyes. He turned over, stretched, and slipped out of bed in one quick motion. Pulling on his jeans and slipping into an ASU T-shirt, he padded down the hall in his bare feet.

Regina was at the stove working on a mess of scrambled eggs. "Good morning," she greeted. "You didn't stay out very late for a Friday night." Aaron dropped onto a chair and leaned his elbows on the table. "What did you do?" she questioned.

"Drove around." He drummed on the tabletop with the tips of his fingers. "I picked up Nick Jerard and one of her friends."

"So you *do* have your eye on Nick."

"I just gave her a ride home. But not before irritating one of her boyfriends. Some Macey guy."

"Todd Macey?"

"Some guy with a very high opinion of himself."

"Sounds like Todd Macey." She checked the biscuits in the oven and announced, "I wasn't going to wake you up. I thought I'd let you sleep. I was going to take the kids in to see Brandon."

"Regina, I'm taking the kids in to Brandon." She kept her back to him. Aaron shook his head. "Regina, take my word for it. The guy's a jerk. A total, absolute jerk."

Regina turned around. "Aaron, don't talk about him like that." She looked away. "I don't know that I could ever trust Brandon again. And yet, I'll start thinking about the good times. I think about the kids and how much they need a dad. I wonder if I should at least give him . . ."

"Regina, I'll take the kids." He pushed himself to his feet and away from the table. She stared at him for a moment. He could see the mist in her eyes, but he couldn't help feeling that the best way to help her was to keep her away from Brandon. Slowly she turned back to the stove.

"Uncle Aaron," Trent asked as they drove toward Brigham City thirty minutes later, "why can't Mom and Dad just work things out?"

"Don't worry about it, big guy," Aaron said gently, ruffling his nephew's blond hair. He felt a sudden pang for these three kids who had been thrown into a mess that they'd never asked for. "Things will work out for you, Trent. You've just got to hang in there. I know it hurts. And it can hurt for quite a while. But it does get better."

He glanced in the backseat at the two girls: Tiffany, three, and Cindy, five. They were seemingly oblivious to what was happening to them. The reality of the family's breakup hadn't affected them totally yet. That would come later. He gripped the steering wheel while the muscles along his jaw tightened. It was at times like this that he despised Brandon because he remembered so vividly what his own father had done to him and his family.

Aaron pulled up to the brick home on the east bench of Brigham City where Brandon lived. It was a home Brandon and Regina had been planning to buy just prior to their separation. Brandon had begun renting there after his break with Regina. Trent and his two sisters piled out and rushed up the front walk as the front door opened and Brandon

Downs came out to greet them. Aaron snatched the girls' sweaters off the backseat, stepped from the Civic, and approached his brother-in-law. "Regina wasn't sure the girls would need these," he said coolly, handing the sweaters to Brandon. "But just in case, you have them."

"Hello, Aaron," Brandon greeted, holding his hand out. "I heard you were up here."

Aaron ignored the outstretched hand for a moment and then shook it. Brandon was a couple of inches taller than Aaron but more slender. His clear blue eyes, blond hair, and straight, even jaw, gave him a poised and confident look. He had always been an impressive figure. But Aaron sensed a hint of submissiveness—even humility—in him today. He was dressed casually in a pair of summer slacks, a bright blue and white Hawaiian shirt, and a pair of beach thongs.

"I thought Regina was going to bring the kids over," Brandon remarked, tousling the girls' hair as they hugged his legs.

Aaron shrugged. "I offered. I'll pick them up this evening."

"I'd like to see Regina. Talk to her."

"Talk to her lawyer, Brandon. That's why she's paying him."

Brandon swallowed and wet his lips. He smiled, dropped down on his haunches, and faced the kids. "Hey, I bought a new video. Why don't you run in and check it out. I'm going to talk to Uncle Aaron for a minute and then we'll head up the canyon."

The kids scrambled into the house and Aaron and Brandon stood facing each other on the front walk. Staring down at the ground, Brandon rubbed the back of his neck with one hand and dug deep in his pants pocket with the other. "I know you won't understand what I'm going to say, Aaron." He shook his head. "I guess I don't expect anyone to understand." He paused, trying to find the right words. "I've been an idiot," he said. "Over the past few weeks I've tried to sort through all the pieces, unscramble all the reasons and lies. I wish I could find a thread of logic to everything. There's nothing. I don't have any excuse. I hate myself for what I've done to Regina and the kids."

"You should."

Brandon looked at Aaron. "I just want to talk to Regina. Everything that's happened so far has been through the two lawyers. She wanted it that way. I understand. But things are different now."

"You feeling the financial pinch?"

For a moment he didn't answer. Then he shook his head. "It's not the money, Aaron. She can have what she wants."

Aaron smiled. "That's big of you, considering she probably doesn't want much of yours. She just wants you out of her life. For good."

"Is that what she told you?"

"Take my word for it."

"I can't accept that, Aaron. I want to talk to her. I don't make excuses for myself. But during the last few weeks I've tried to make some real changes in my life. I've seen Bishop Sutter and President Francis."

"That's good."

"It hasn't been easy. I have a long way to go to make it back."

"Plan on crawling back without Regina. She doesn't need the extra baggage. Do her a favor and stay out of her life."

"I can do that. But I have to know if that's what she really wants. Will you tell her I want to talk to her?"

Aaron's face color deepened and his eyes darkened in anger. For a moment it appeared he would explode.

Gradually he conquered his emotions and spoke. "Let me tell you something about Regina you've apparently forgotten." Aaron cleared his throat and stared up at the mountains that towered behind Brandon's home.

"When Regina was twelve, her old man pulled the same crap that you've pulled on her. He ran off. It's not easy to be abandoned by your father when you're twelve, just when everything's changing inside you and around you. You don't need that kind of trauma in your life right then. Well, Regina didn't have a chance to worry about herself. She was worrying about her nine-year-old brother, who was losing it. She held me together during that time.

"Later you came along. In a lot of ways you pulled her through. You gave her somebody to lean on, someone to trust, so she wouldn't ever have to worry about being abandoned again. Maybe if her dad had stayed around, she wouldn't have needed you so much. But he didn't. She would have done anything for you. Anything. And how do you repay her? She gets dumped on again, just like before. She deserved more from you. You're not going to trample on her again. I don't care how sorry you feel."

"What your father did to you and Regina—"

"Jack Solinski is my father, not AJ Tippets," Aaron snapped. "I don't even know where AJ Tippets is. Or whether he's dead or alive. And that suits me fine. The sooner Regina feels that way about you, the better off she'll be."

Brandon held up his hands. "Okay, I can accept the fact that Regina might want me out of her life. I can't blame her. But I want her to be the one to tell me."

"Brandon, you need to know one thing: I'm up here because of Regina. There are plenty of construction jobs down in Phoenix. I didn't have to drive eight hundred miles to find a place that would let me drive their dump truck.

Regina pulled me through seventeen years ago. I'm returning the favor. Seventeen years ago, I wanted to be big
enough, strong enough, and mean enough to settle a score
with AJ Tippets. But I wasn't. Things have changed,
though, Brandon. Don't stop by while I'm around."

Brandon smiled sadly. "Aaron, I know that on my best
day and your worst, I wouldn't stand a chance against you.
My fight isn't with you. It's with myself. But I'm going to see
Regina. Even if I have to go to blows with you. I love her.
You won't believe that. Maybe she won't believe it. I didn't
believe it. But it's true."

"I'll pick the kids up this evening. Seven o'clock sharp."

"Can you make it eight-thirty? We've got a big day
planned."

"All right, eight-thirty. If for any reason I'm late, you
wait for me. Because I'll be here."

As Aaron climbed into the Civic, revved the engine,
and sped away, he noticed his hands were perspiring and
that he had a knot in his stomach. It wasn't until he had
driven several miles that he was able to loosen his grip on
the wheel and relax. Strangely enough he began to think
about Nick and her overprotective brothers.

Chapter Five

Aaron didn't mention his visit with Brandon to Regina. For the biggest part of the day he kept to himself, but toward evening he took a long walk. He had no destination in mind but found himself walking out of town toward the river bottom where the old bridge spanned the muddy waters of the Bear River.

The bridge was about forty yards or so in length, an old metal structure set on rock and cement pilings. It was only wide enough for a single vehicle to cross at a time, and there was a weight limit of fifteen tons.

Aaron strolled onto the bridge, where the asphalt pavement was cracking and crumbling. Ambling to the middle, he leaned against the rusted cables that served as guardrails. He stared down into the murky water fifteen feet below as it sluggishly swirled about the pilings under him and formed a series of whirlpools just downriver from the bridge.

The banks of the river were steep, thickly covered with grass, brush, and weeds. The day's heat was gradually giving way to a more comfortable mildness, and already the shadows from the west bank were drenching the river-bottom in shade. A cow bawled occasionally in the distance, and the drone of a far-off tractor engine just made it more peaceful. Aaron picked up a couple of asphalt fragments and dropped them into the water.

In the midst of his quiet meditation, a jogger came over

the hill and into view. He watched as she made her way along the road and then turned onto the bridge. As she drew closer, he recognized Nick.

Wearing an oversized white and blue USU football T-shirt and a pair of navy blue, silky running shorts, she ran effortlessly, with a smooth, elongated stride. She had on a beige, long-billed, tight-fitting baseball cap and her pony-tail, which was threaded through the hole in the back of her cap, danced rhythmically as she ran.

She didn't notice Aaron until she was well onto the bridge. When she did see him, her concentration broke, her face relaxed into a smile, and she pulled up next to him.

"What're you doing way out here?" she asked, putting her hands on her hips and breathing deeply. "Waiting for a full moon?"

Aaron stuffed his hands into his back pockets and looked around. "Well," he drawled, pursing his lips, "I was waiting for a beautiful girl to come jogging out of the sunset."

Nick laughed. "Fat chance. Maybe a stray cow if you're lucky." She stared across the bridge to the opposite bank and brushed the back of her hand across her perspiring forehead. "Well, let me know if you have any luck." She started off.

"Aren't there laws against abandoning strangers on lonely country bridges? I might get run over by a potbellied cow." Without turning around, she waved. "Are you coming back this way?" Aaron called after her.

"It's the only way across the river. Unless I swim."

"Don't swim. Take the bridge," he yelled.

Aaron watched her go up the far bank and disappear from sight over the hill and into a stand of poplar trees. Twenty minutes later she emerged from the poplars and dropped back into the river bottom. She smiled when she saw him still there.

Slowing up at the edge of the bridge, she walked the last fifty feet to where he was leaning against the bridge cables. "No luck with the beautiful girl?" she asked, smiling through gulps of air.

He picked up a pebble and tossed it into the water. "None of them was my type."

"Walk with me," Nick suggested, laughing. "If I don't keep walking my legs get tight."

"Do you run often?" Aaron asked, walking beside her.

"Every day. Except Sundays."

"You some kind of health nut or something?"

"Or something." She laughed. "I went to USU on a volleyball scholarship. In my third game I messed up my knee and was out for the rest of the season. As soon as I was able, I started jogging to get back into shape."

"So this is how a country girl gets her kicks. She goes out and runs a couple of miles."

"Five to be exact."

"Five? I'm impressed."

Nick smiled. "Last spring I was jogging at the track. The track coach saw me and thought I might be able to make the team as a walk-on."

"And volleyball?"

She shrugged. "I think I've got a chance in the 1500 meters or something a little longer."

"You're a genuine jock?"

She shrugged. "I played volleyball, basketball, and softball in high school. What else could I do with six coaching brothers?"

"And now they want you to be a track star?"

She shook her head. "They think I should settle down and forget all the sports stuff. Especially Jared. He's afraid I'm going to scare the right guy off."

"Meaning Richard Rawlins?"

"*Robbins*," she corrected.

"Right. I knew that."

She grinned. "Richard is the academic type. Not that I'm not. But I enjoy a little more activity than I get from turning textbook pages."

"Does your being a jock scare Richard?"

"I haven't asked him. Besides," she added emphatically, "Richard and I are just friends—contrary to what my brothers might believe."

Aaron was surprised that they had walked the mile to the Jerard place so quickly. "I better head back. I didn't expect to go so far." He looked down at his watch. "I've got to pick Regina's kids up in a bit."

"I'll give you a ride."

Aaron started to protest, but before he could say anything, Nick was off to the house for the keys to the pickup.

"Hey, what's happening?" someone called out.

Aaron turned to see Jared coming from a shed, carrying a shovel over his shoulder.

"I was out walking and your sister almost ran me over. I walked her home."

Jared set the shovel down and leaned on it. "I wish she'd get over this running kick."

"She might be good."

"Would you think twice about a girl who goes out and runs five miles a day and wants to make the USU track team as a walk-on?"

Aaron grinned. "Maybe. If I could beat her in a race."

"You probably couldn't beat Nick." He wagged his head.

"Ready?" Nick asked as she jogged up with the keys.

"Maybe Aaron will go with us to the young adult party," Jared remarked casually. "It's just a gathering in the city park over by the church. They're frying hamburgers, playing games."

"Do you want to come?" Nick asked.

"I've got to pick up Regina's kids at eight-thirty."

"Drop by later. We'll save you something to eat," Jared said. Glancing at Nick, he added, "We're certainly not going to be very early ourselves considering that Nick's still dressed for a track meet."

"I'll try to make it," Aaron said.

Regina was busy baking cookies when Aaron came in. "Where have you been?" she called over her shoulder.

"Just wandering. It's about time I picked up the kids."

"Brandon called and said the kids were fed. He offered to bring them, but I told him you were emphatic about picking them up yourself."

"Did he talk to you much?" Aaron asked irritably.

She turned to the sink and started scrubbing a pan. "We talked a while."

"Regina, I'm not trying to be a repetitive royal pain, but you don't need him."

She laughed. "Brandon did say you were pretty protective this morning." She turned and faced him, her hands dripping. "I appreciate you, Aaron. I really do."

"What did he want? Obviously more than to let you know the kids were ready to come home." She didn't answer, turning back to the sink and continuing her scrubbing. "Regina, what did he say?"

"He asked me out to dinner at Maddox."

"When?"

"Next Friday."

"You're not going, are you?"

"I told him I needed to think about it."

"Does that mean yes?" Regina didn't answer. "I'll pick up the kids," he muttered, turning away and heading for the door.

"Aaron." He stopped with his back to her. "I'm going to be careful. He wanted to take me out tonight. I suggested next Friday. I told him I wouldn't go before then. I want time to get myself ready—ready mentally. I won't have any illusions. I'm going to look carefully before I take a step."

"Would you consider going back to him?"

"I still love him. I have to admit that. But there's a lot of hurt, a lot of disappointment."

"But you could change your mind, is that it?"

"Aaron, I need you. I appreciate you. I know you want to help me." He could tell she was crying. He couldn't bring himself to turn around and face her. Seeing her tears would only make him more angry. "But, Aaron, I have to make this decision myself."

Aaron was curt and cold when he picked up the three kids. They came laughing and screaming out of the house and piled into the Civic, chattering about everything they had done that day—picnicking up the canyon, hiking, wading in a stream, throwing frisbees.

"Thanks for picking them up," Brandon said.

Aaron had hardly acknowledged him until then, paying attention to the kids so he wouldn't have to face his brother-in-law. "You didn't have to call. You knew I was going to pick them up."

Brandon nodded. "I told you this morning I wanted to talk to your sister."

Aaron started for the car.

"Aaron," Brandon called after him. "I'll make you a promise." Aaron faced him. "Maybe I don't deserve Regina and Trent and Cindy and Tiffany. But I want to deserve them some day. I promise you I won't hurt Regina." He swallowed. "If I hurt her, you're welcome to come here and bust me in the mouth. That's a promise."

"You've made lots of promises to Regina. Some of them

over the altar. They haven't done her much good." He
scowled. "But I'll take you up on it. And I'll do more than
bust you in the mouth."

Aaron was still angry by the time he drove up to the city
park in Bear River City. He had debated about going at all,
but he needed something to get his mind off Brandon and
Regina.

The park was small, located just east of the church on
Main Street. There was a ball diamond, a kiddie playground,
and a bowery with a half dozen picnic tables.

"You made it," Nick called out as Aaron strolled across
the lawn toward where she was frying hamburgers. She was
dressed in a pair of bleached jeans and a buttoned, red,
western-style shirt. She had kicked off her shoes and was
walking around in her bare feet. She was pretty.

"I wondered if you'd show," she said as he drew closer.

Aaron looked about self-consciously and stuffed his
shirttails in his pants. "What can I say? I got hungry."

Nick gave him a playful shove. "Well, let's do something
about the growl in your stomach. Grab a plate. I'll fix you a
hamburger while you load up with salad and chips."

Aaron looked about. There were a couple of dozen
young adults, some eating, some playing volleyball, a few
throwing horseshoes. Everything was pretty casual. He
loaded his plate and picked up his hamburger from Nick.
She found him a place at one of the picnic tables and sat
down next to him.

As he sat munching his dinner and visiting with Nick,
Theresa Porter stepped over to where they were sitting and
said, "Todd Macey just drove up."

Nick looked annoyed. "Why doesn't he take a hint?"
Turning to Aaron, she said, "Don't worry about Todd."

Turning back to Theresa, she asked, "Where are Jared and Joshua?"

"Jared's playing horseshoes. I haven't seen Joshua."

"What's the sweat?" Aaron asked, more curious than anxious.

"You remember the guy you pushed down last night? He's here."

Aaron smiled. "I'm not going to push him down again." He laughed. "As far as I'm concerned that's over and done with."

"Todd may not see it that way."

Before Nick could go for her brothers, Todd Macey sauntered up to the group with two of his friends. All three of them wore boots and jeans. Todd was squeezed into a white muscle shirt.

"So this is where we find the big man," Todd sneered across the table at Aaron. "Stuffing his face." Aaron continued eating, hardly looking up. "Maybe you want to start where we left off?" Todd challenged. "Maybe this time you won't run off."

"Maybe this time you won't fall all over yourself." Aaron smiled, taking another huge bite of hamburger.

The forced smile disappeared from Todd's face. He stared coldly across the table. "You name the time and place."

"I'm not looking for anything, Macey," Aaron answered calmly, chewing his food.

Todd nodded his head. "You keep looking over your shoulder, because I'm coming for you one of these days. This is your wake-up call." He started away.

"Don't trip over the curb rushing off," Aaron called.

Nick looked in horror, first at Aaron and then at Todd. Todd had his back to Aaron, but slowly he turned, his face pinched with anger. "I don't believe I caught that," he said huskily.

Aaron smiled disarmingly. "So you're deaf, too?"

"You're really looking for it, aren't you?"

"Macey, I'm not looking for anything. You're the one who strutted in here looking for some place to shove your face." He shrugged indifferently. "Just don't shove it in my direction, and we'll both be happy."

Slowly Todd came around the table. Nick jumped up and met him halfway. "Stop it!" she shouted, blocking his path.

"He's the one pushing it," Todd growled, jabbing a finger in Aaron's direction.

"Nobody asked you here," she said.

"I thought this was an open party."

"Not so you could come and pick a fight."

Jared and Joshua pushed through the small group that had gathered. Quietly they moved between Todd and Nick. "If you want to stay and eat and have fun, you're welcome," Jared offered. "But there isn't going to be any trouble."

"You speaking for him?" Todd asked, nodding his head in Aaron's direction.

"We're not having any trouble."

Todd looked past Jared and Joshua. His eyes locked onto Aaron's. "This doesn't finish anything."

Aaron returned the stare without speaking. Todd muttered something to his two friends, and the three of them turned and headed across the park to their car. An electric tension left with them.

"Thanks," Nick said huskily to her two brothers. She turned back to Aaron. "You all right?"

Aaron looked down at himself and began to feel himself. "No broken bones. I'm still in one piece."

"You're lucky," Jared remarked.

Aaron laughed out loud. "I can handle myself."

"You don't know Todd Macey." Jared smiled, shaking his head. "I'm glad things didn't get mean. Macey's always looking for his next fight. If there's one thing he does better than ride bulls, it's fight. Don't mess with him."

"Thanks for the warning." Aaron smiled and returned to his food.

"Jared and Joshua were trying to help you," Nick sputtered beside him as her brothers walked away shaking their heads.

"I guess I'm not used to having a couple of nursemaids. I didn't grow up with six brothers to watch out for me."

"If you think that just because you managed to push Todd down once when he was off guard that you can take care of him, you're mistaken. You should be glad Jared and Joshua were here."

"If it's all the same to you and your brothers," Aaron answered steadily, "I'll take care of myself. Even against your famous bull rider."

She stiffened, glaring at him. Suddenly she turned and stomped off to the grill, leaving him alone. He watched her go. Slowly he pushed his plate away from him, stood, and headed across the park to his car.

"You're back early," Regina greeted him as he came in the door and dropped into the recliner in the living room. Regina sat curled up on the sofa in her nightgown and robe with a novel in her lap.

Slumping in the recliner, Aaron closed his eyes and stretched. "What a bummer," he muttered under his breath.

"Wasn't there anyone there who interested you? I thought you said Nick was going."

"She was there."

"And?"

Aaron rubbed his eyes with the balls of his hands. "So was Todd Macey."

"Nick was with Todd?"

"No, but Macey tried to pick a fight with me," he groaned. "Nick's brothers jumped in to save my life."

"And?" Regina prompted again.

"She got all bent out of shape because I wasn't the epitome of gratitude."

"They were probably just trying to help."

Aaron sat up and leaned forward with his forearms on his knees. Nodding, he answered. "I know. I was just in a lousy mood." He laughed humorlessly. "I've been stepping on everybody's toes today. The last thing I needed was for Todd Macey to stick his face into mine."

"If it will make you feel any better, Trent just went to bed. He asked if you were going to be home to tuck him in. I told him not to count on it tonight."

Smiling, Aaron pushed himself to his feet. "Well, it's good to know that someone isn't sore at me. If anybody can put me in a good mood, Trent can." He started down the hall to the bedroom. "But with my luck," he added, "he'll already be asleep."

He pushed open the bedroom door a crack and peeked in. "Hi, Uncle Aaron. I heard your car pull in."

Aaron flipped on a lamp sitting on the dresser. "How are you, tiger," he grinned, dropping down on the edge of the bed and slapping Trent playfully about the head. Trent ducked under the covers. Then for a moment the two were together, just smiling and staring at each other.

"I'm sure glad you're here, Uncle Aaron. Especially since Dad's not here right now."

Aaron studied his nephew. His blond hair was long in the back and clipped short around the ears. His bright, sparkling, blue eyes were framed in long, thick lashes. He was almost too fine featured for a boy. Aaron could see a lot of Brandon in him.

"How did things go today, kid?"

"It was awesome!" He took a deep breath and pushed his head deeper into his pillow. "You know, a while back I didn't like visiting Dad. I had a funny feeling when I went there. But the last few times it's been different. I wish Dad would come home. He said maybe he will. What do you think, Uncle Aaron?"

Aaron began wiping wrinkles from the bedspread. "Oh, I don't know. That will have to be up to your mom and dad. But don't expect anything."

"Dad's not a bad guy, is he?"

Aaron rubbed his chin pensively. "He's made some mistakes."

"I know. He even said so today. He said he was sorry. You like Dad, don't you?"

Aaron laughed. "Look, kid, tomorrow's Sunday. You won't be able to get up for church. Stop asking so many questions and get to sleep. And don't think so much. Things'll work out."

Chapter Six

Monday evening as Nick jogged across the Bear River bridge, she was surprised to see Aaron standing on the bridge, dressed in sweatpants, a T-shirt, and running shoes. She stopped a few feet from him and stared.

"I figured I'd jog with you," Aaron said, bending over to stretch his legs.

"I thought you were mad."

Aaron shrugged. "Who said I'm not?" he said seriously and then flashed a smile. "You're the one who walked away mad Saturday night."

"You were rude." She took a deep breath. "You didn't say anything to me at church yesterday."

"You were sitting on the other side of the chapel. I didn't want to shout."

"I could tell you were still mad. Maybe I'm still mad too."

Aaron shrugged. "I can still jog with you, can't I?"

"I thought you said you don't like to jog."

"I don't. But I'll give it a try."

"I doubt you can keep up." She continued across the bridge, jogging.

Aaron fell in beside her stride for stride.

"I like running alone," Nick remarked. "Nobody else can keep up with me. And running gives me a chance to think."

"If I can't keep up, leave me. I'm trying to stay in shape.

54

Just like you. And I won't talk. That way you can still think."

"You're already talking too much."

The conversation stopped as the two started up the incline from the river bottom and proceeded at a steady pace down the flat country road. On either side of them were fields of corn, wheat, barley, and alfalfa. It was late enough in the day that the heat had begun to let up, but it was still warm enough that both runners were soon sweating profusely.

"I make a complete loop," Nick announced. "We cross the river twice. The complete loop is a little over five miles. I pick up my pace on the final stretch."

The strain was beginning to tell on Aaron. He was sucking in air and his face was darkened by the heat and the strain. "Don't pamper me."

"I was warning you."

By the time the two of them reached the bridge again, Aaron was several paces behind, but he hadn't given up. Nick pulled up at the bridge and waited for Aaron to catch up. When he did, the two of them began to walk and shake their muscles loose.

"I didn't think you could do it," Nick commented after a moment. "None of my brothers can keep up with me." She laughed. "Maybe that's why they don't like to see me run. They don't want to be shown up."

Aaron closed his eyes, put his head back and took huge gulps of air. "I used to be an old track star myself," he gasped. "I've got a stubborn streak, too. I'd have died before I would have let you leave me too far behind."

"You look like you're about ready to die right now. I stopped to give you a rest. I usually don't stop until I reach the house. That's another mile."

"You bragging or just trying to make me feel bad?" Aaron said, beginning to breathe a little easier.

"A little of both."

Aaron nodded and wet his lips. "How are you in a sprint?"

Nick grinned, sensing a challenge. "Distance is what I do best. But there aren't many guys who can beat me in a sprint. Only Joseph and James can take me in the hundred or the two hundred meters. On a good day I might beat them."

"Maybe I could beat them on my bad days."

"Don't count on it."

"How far would you say it is across the river bottom here?"

Nick studied the distance between the two banks, which was spanned by the bridge in the middle. "Eighty, maybe a hundred yards of flat road before the road goes up the banks."

"That's close enough." He started back to the north bank. "I'll give you ten yards," he called over his shoulder.

Nick laughed. "If I run, I run as an equal."

"Humor me this time. Take ten yards. I like a challenge."

Nick followed after him. He began lining up. She stepped next to him.

"Take ten yards," he ordered. "You'll need them."

She stared at him, just a little peeved. "All right. I'll take them." She took two steps forward.

"Take a little more."

She glowered at him and took two more short steps. "I hope you're not one of those sensitive male types who can't stand to have a girl beat him."

"Oh, I'm very sensitive. That's why I'm giving you a headstart. I figure I've got to be fair with you."

"I'm not afraid to humiliate a guy. I'm very competitive, and if I can beat you, I will."

"You can't."

Nick turned forward and prepared herself for the start. Her jaw was set, her body tense, her eyes staring down at the pavement. Behind her, Aaron prepared himself, and when he was ready he gave the signal.

The two of them bolted forward, their legs reaching out and lapping up the yards, their arms churning smoothly, rhythmically, both running to win. At the halfway point Aaron was a stride behind Nick. When they reached the finish point, he was two strides in front of her.

"I can beat my brothers some of the time," she protested, staring at Aaron in disbelief and taking great gulps of air as she paced with her hands on her hips.

Breathing hard, Aaron jogged back to the bridge. "I can beat your brothers *every* time," he remarked over his shoulder smiling broadly.

"Let's try it again."

Aaron laughed. "The only way you can beat me is to take a bigger headstart."

"Don't be so sure."

"But I *am* sure. That's why I raced you. You don't think I would have set up a race so a girl could beat me, do you? You see, I'm very competitive. And sensitive about being humiliated by a girl."

They didn't speak again for several minutes. When Nick finally said something, the two of them were on the bridge, leaning their forearms on the cable and staring down into the murky water below. "You're a sprinter?"

Aaron smiled. "I was once."

"How good were you?"

"The girls didn't beat me."

"That doesn't tell me anything."

Aaron pushed away from the railing. "I'll walk you home."

"How good were you?" Nick persisted.

"What difference does it make?"

"I don't want to get beaten by a slouch."

"As a senior I was shooting for the state record in the 100 and 200 meters. There was only one guy in the whole state who stood in the way of me and those two state championships. A guy from Westwood in Mesa. A week before the divisional meet, we had a dual meet with Westwood. Unfortunately, this other guy was ineligible.

"I won in both the 100 and the 200 that day, but it didn't mean anything. The kid was even there. He wanted to race against me as much as I wanted to race against him. So after the meet the two of us went against each other in the 100." Aaron smiled and shook his head. "We both wanted to know. Our coaches lined us up. We did everything by the rules. It just didn't count.

"And?"

"Both of us broke the state record. I beat him by half a hair." He shrugged. "Two days later I smashed up on my three-wheeler. No broken bones or anything, just a lot of scrapes and bruises. I couldn't compete in the state meet. The guy from Westwood won in both the 100 and the 200. But he didn't beat my time."

"You didn't try track in college?"

"I didn't even try college. Not back then."

"I don't feel so bad."

"You'd hate to get beat by some ordinary guy, is that it?"

Nick cocked her head to one side and shrugged. "You might say that. I could still beat you in the mile."

"How about a half-mile?" Aaron asked.

"I could beat you in a half-mile."

"Would you give me a headstart? Say fifty yards?"

"I'll give you a hundred."

"I'm no slouch," he reminded her.

"I'll give you a hundred and ten."

Aaron laughed and shook his head. "You sound too confident. I'll quit while I'm ahead."

Nick started jogging and Aaron followed. They didn't say anything until they arrived at Nick's place. "I'll give you a ride home," Nick offered.

"I'll take you up on your offer. I haven't been looking forward to a jog back home."

They rode in silence for a while and then Aaron spoke. "You know what you need, Nick?"

She looked over at him. "What do I need?"

"A coach."

"A coach?"

Aaron nodded.

"And I suppose you're humbly recommending yourself?"

"Of course. Do you know anybody else who is better? Or anybody who would put up with your feminine superiority?"

"I know a few who are a little more humble."

"Since when was humility the sterling quality of a good coach?"

"I've got six coaches."

"But they want to coach you in everything but track."

Nick grinned over at Aaron who sat slumped down in his seat with his arm out the window and his dark hair blowing in the wind. "You're crazy," she said.

"Now," Aaron said, raising a portentous index finger, "being crazy *is* a necessary trait of a good coach. Do I have the job?"

"I'll meet you at my place tomorrow night at seven-thirty."

Aaron shook his head. "You don't understand."

"What?"

"We'll meet at the bridge tomorrow at 7:45. I'm the coach. I call the shots."

"On second thought, I'm not sure I want you for my coach."

The next evening the two showed up at the bridge, Nick on foot and Aaron on his sister's ten-speed.

"That's not fair," Nick protested when she saw him. "I thought we were both going to run."

"Since when do you tell your coach what you're going to do?"

"But I thought—"

"We'll start out with five miles."

After the five miles Aaron gave her a chance to catch her breath, and then he paced her in a series of windsprints at the bridge.

"Why am I doing all this sprinting?" Nick gasped, sweat pouring down her face. "I mean, I'm trying to be a distance runner, not play halfback for the Denver Broncos."

"It gets you in shape. And when you come down that last stretch, you're going to want to kick into a higher gear. Take my word for it."

When the workout was finished, Nick was bent over, her hands on her knees, trying to catch her breath while Aaron sat comfortably astride his bike and remarked, "You know, you need something to shoot for."

"I'm trying to make the USU track team as a walk-on," Nick muttered.

"You need something more immediate." Aaron thought for a moment. "There's a 10K in two weeks in Logan. I heard about it on the radio."

"I've never run a 10K."

"This will be a new challenge. I expect you to be one of the top finishers."

"I didn't say whether I wanted to do it."

"I didn't ask you. I'm the coach. I don't *ask* you any-thing."

"You can be fired, you know."

Aaron grinned, climbing off his bike and leaning it against the bridge. "I'll humor you, Nick. I'll jog with you to your place."

Nick rolled her eyes. "You're all heart, *Coach*."

When they jogged into the yard a few minutes later, Jared was lounging under a tree in a lawn chair. Nick col-lapsed down beside him while Aaron stood panting a few steps away.

"We might make a runner out of her yet," Aaron com-mented, glancing down at Nick.

Nick rolled her eyes again and shook her head. She nod-ded toward Aaron and grumbled, "Meet my new coach. If I had known he was going to take this thing so seriously, I wouldn't have given him the time of day."

"Some day you're going to care more about making a decent meal than you are about making the track team," Jared observed.

"Right now I want to run. And besides, you haven't complained too much about my cooking. Have you ever considered that I can be good at both?"

Both brother and sister looked at Aaron as though solic-iting his opinion to break the impasse. He took a step back-ward and held up his hands. "Don't look at me. I'm not going to get into any family squabble. I'm just the coach."

"Chicken," Nick said, pushing herself to her feet and heading toward the house.

"Same time tomorrow," Aaron called after her.

"Why don't you take her out to some fancy restaurant and make a lady out of her," Jared asked as Nick went into the house.

"She's already a lady. I'm surprised you haven't noticed. But she can be a successful runner, too. She's good, you know. She's got the legs for it. And the determination."

"Richard Robbins isn't going to be interested in marrying a track star."

Aaron laughed. "Nick might not be interested in marrying a doctor." He shrugged. "I've got to get going."

"For crying out loud, Solinski, when I told you to get a date with her, I didn't mean a jogging date."

"I'm her track coach, not her beau," he called over his shoulder.

"Did I tell you that Todd Macey's on the prowl?"

Aaron stopped and turned.

"He's got it in for you. He's not real happy with Joshua and me either, but he's smart enough to know that if he messes with one of us, he's got to mess with all of us. Not even Macey's that dumb."

"Thanks for the warning."

Chapter Seven

"How do I look?" Regina asked nervously as she came down the hall and into the kitchen. Aaron was sitting at the table finishing a glass of milk and a peanut butter and jam sandwich. Her cheeks were flushed and her eyes clouded with worry. Wearing a light-weight, flowered, cotton dress and low heels, she fidgeted in the doorway and waited for her brother's verdict.

Aaron looked her over. Her short, brown hair gave her a young, girlish look. But she was pretty. Even being her brother, he could see that. Pulling the corners of his mouth down into a frown, he muttered, "I guess you look all right. Good enough for who you're going with." Then he grinned teasingly. "Actually, you look great. I just wish you had someone decent to go with."

"Aaron, don't say any more." She pressed her hands to her cheeks and closed her eyes. "I can't believe I'm this nervous. You'd think I didn't even know him."

"I'm not sure you do." Heaving a sigh, he took his empty glass to the sink. "But I'll keep my mouth shut."

"There are a lot of things you don't understand."

"Especially where you and Brandon are concerned."

"This is something I've got to do." She nervously pressed her lips together. "I've done a lot of thinking this past week. I can always push for the divorce. But first I have to make sure there's nothing left worth saving. If there is something

63

there . . . " She didn't finish. She stepped to the window and glanced out.

"Sit down and relax."

"Will you answer the door when he comes? And be civil?"

Aaron folded his arms and leaned against the kitchen counter. "Regina, I think you're making a big mistake, but if this is what you want to do, I'm not going to stop you. And I'll be civil. Against my will."

"I hate having you stay at home with the kids on a Friday night."

"I volunteered, and we're not staying home. We're going to the park. Stop worrying."

The sound of a car pulling into the driveway ended their conversation. Regina stood statue-like. Aaron stepped to the window, cracked the curtains, and peered out. "He's here. I'll catch the door."

"I'll be in my room."

"Keep him waiting a little bit. You don't want him to think you're too eager. Not on your first date."

Aaron let Brandon knock twice before he opened the door.

"Hello, Brandon."

"Hello, Aaron."

For a moment Aaron blocked the doorway; then slowly he stepped aside and motioned with a sweep of his hand for Brandon to enter. "Have a seat. Regina will be with you in just a minute. Regina," he called down the hall, "Brandon's here."

It was five minutes before Regina appeared. When she did, Brandon scrambled to his feet. "Hello, Regina." He wet his lips and stared at her. "You look nice." He grinned. "You look really nice."

"I know you two aren't used to a curfew, but since I'm

playing daddy this evening, I get to say it. Remember, midnight's the magic hour."

"Thanks, Daddy," Regina cut him off.

From the living room window Aaron watched them walk to the car. They didn't hold hands or touch, but Brandon opened the door for her. Aaron turned away, going to the back door and calling to the three kids, who were playing in the backyard. "Hey, guys, you ready to ride over to the park?"

"Has Daddy come?" Trent called.

"Come and gone."

"And he didn't even tell us hello?"

"He came to see your mom."

"Will we get to see him when he comes home?"

"You'll be sawing logs by then. Let's go."

The three kids piled into the Civic with Aaron, and he drove over to the Bear River City park. Aaron pushed them in the swings, sent them down the slide, played kickball, and ran races with them across the grass. They ended up in a pile with Aaron on the bottom and the three kids laughing and crawling on him.

"So there really are four kids playing over here," someone called from the fence. Aaron was lying face down on the lawn, and he rolled over to see who was speaking.

"Nick!" Cindy squealed, jumping up and rushing to the fence where Nick and Theresa were both leaning, smiling. "Come and play. Uncle Aaron will let you."

"I take it you two have met," Aaron commented as Cindy climbed into Nick's arms and squeezed her neck.

"I've been babysitting Cindy since she was two weeks old. We're practically family. We were driving by," Nick went on, "and we saw these kids playing in the park like they were crazy. One of them was so big we thought that—"

"You're never too old to play in the park," Aaron said. "Come in and join us. We need a couple more people to get a really good game of kickball going. Or do you have other, more pressing plans?"

"No, we were just driving around, thinking about driving down to Ogden or something."

"Oh, so you weren't out hitchhiking this weekend?"

"We might play kickball with you," Nick offered, "if you let us know how the teams will be divided."

"Trent and I will stand all the girls. And the losers buy treats for the winners."

"I hope you have lots of money," Nick laughed.

The six of them played until it started to get dark. The score ended up twenty-seven to eighteen in favor of the girls.

"We can't stop now," Trent protested when they all collapsed as darkness settled around them. "We can't let girls beat us."

"When they flat out whip you, you have to be a good loser," Aaron laughed, ruffling Trent's blond hair. "I'd hate to keep playing. I'm afraid they'd run up the score on us."

"We want our treats," Cindy piped up with a grin.

"Where's a good place around here to buy a treat?" Aaron asked, pushing himself to his feet.

"Let's go over to the Honeyville store," Nick offered.

"Where's that?"

"Honeyville's just across the river a couple of miles, up next to the mountain. It's just a little place. Not much there except a couple of gas stations, a post office, school, church, and store. Jeremiah used to take me over there all the time for popsicles or soda pops."

"Let's head for the famous Honeyville country store then," Aaron said. "We'll take the Civic."

"Can we all get in?" Nick asked.

"Don't worry. We'll squeeze everybody in."

The store was tiny with a western facade. There was a narrow boardwalk in front and a couple of gas pumps between the store and the road. Inside, there were a half dozen shelves, crammed with bread, chips, and canned goods. It had a definite country flavor to it.

The three kids quickly found the candy shelves and the soda pop cooler. Everyone ended up with a soda pop and a small bag of dime candy.

Once outside, the group took a short walk in the dark up the street to the elementary school. Theresa and the three kids hurried ahead while Nick and Aaron hung back, sipping their drinks and talking.

"Cindy was saying that her mom and dad went out this evening."

Aaron nodded and took a drink of his root beer.

"Are they getting back together?"

"I hope Regina's smarter than that. I've tried to talk to her, but I suspect she's made up her mind to give Brandon another chance. I think she's setting herself up for another fall. This one worse than the last."

"I think Brandon's changed, Aaron."

"Changed?" Aaron looked over at Nick. "Do you know what he did to her?"

Nick drank the last swallow of her strawberry soda. "Aaron, I've been here the whole time. There isn't anybody outside my own family I like as much as I do Regina. She was my Merrie Miss teacher and my Laurel teacher. There isn't a better person in the whole world. Jeremiah was telling me just the other day that Brandon's working hard to put his life back in order. He's been excommunicated. He wants to make things right. You can't be his judge."

"And you can?"

"Regina can, better than either of us."

"I feel my whole summer will be wasted if she takes him back."

"Because things don't end up the way you think they should?"

Aaron shrugged and rolled his pop bottle between his hands. "Maybe."

"You can't live Regina's life for her."

"But I don't have to stand by while she gets hurt again."

"She's not going to rush into anything. Give her credit for some intelligence."

"Her feelings are all wrapped around her intelligence. That's what I worry about."

Nick stopped and looked down at her empty pop bottle. "I remember how things were with Brandon and Regina. Before all this other stuff happened. They were happy." She looked up. "When I was a little girl, I wanted to have a marriage just like theirs. Maybe they can still have that. Maybe that's what Regina is thinking. You're thinking about all the bad things that Brandon has done to her in the last few months. Maybe Regina is remembering the years before that, when life was a lot better for her."

"And you want her to forget the bad?"

"I want her to do what she feels like she has to do. Maybe she's willing to forgive. If she is, that shouldn't trouble us."

It was after ten-thirty by the time Aaron had the three kids in bed. He wandered into the living room and dropped on the sofa, debating whether to turn on the TV and catch the tail end of the news or to give up and go to bed himself. For thirty minutes he sat motionless, staring into the darkness, trying to sort through his feelings and thoughts.

A car pulled up. Two doors opened and closed. He heard muffled voices, a little bit of laughter, silence, voices, silence again, and then the front door opened and Regina walked in smiling. She snapped on the light in the hall and spotted Aaron on the sofa.

"You're not waiting up for me, are you?" she asked cheerily. She pushed the door closed behind her and walked over to the love seat and sank into it.

Aaron made a show of looking at his watch. "It's 11:18."

"I made curfew." She laughed, slumped down, leaned her head against the back of the love seat and closed her eyes.

"Well?" Aaron asked after a moment of silence. "How'd it go?"

She breathed in slowly and held her breath for a moment. Exhaling, she answered, "It was okay."

"Regina, *okay* doesn't tell me anything." She smiled without answering. "Look, Regina, I've taken care of the kids. I took them to the park. We had a great time. I bathed them and put them to bed. They're asleep. I've been—"

"Aaron, you're a good daddy. Thanks."

"I don't want a thank-you. I want to know how things went."

Regina sat up. "I'd better get to bed." She stood up. "I've got to get up early tomorrow."

"Regina!"

"Brandon's picking the kids and me up at seven. We're going to Salt Lake to the zoo."

Aaron stared at her. "Things were more than just okay?"

"We had a good talk."

"You're taking him back?"

She shook her head. "We haven't decided anything. He's changed, Aaron. But I don't know yet what's going to happen."

"Did you do anything but hold hands?"

She laughed. "That's pretty abrupt and personal."

"Remember I'm playing Daddy tonight. I have a right to ask."

"Everybody has a right to ask. But you don't always have a right to an answer." Smiling, she started down the hall to her room. A moment later she poked her head back into the living room and said, "Yes, he did kiss me. You should have been at the window and you might have seen the last one. But don't let your imagination run away with you."

With Regina and the kids gone, Aaron spent Saturday alone, working on the '57 Chevy. Even though he stayed busy, his thoughts kept turning to Nick. He considered several excuses for dropping by her place, but none of them seemed legitimate, and he didn't want to come across as too anxious, especially if Nick saw him as just another friend. In the evening he took a shower, ate leftovers, and endured an inane TV movie before going to bed early.

Sunday morning was beautiful, clean, and invigorating, with the refreshing scent of newly cut alfalfa hay hanging in the air. Everything was green and alive as Aaron walked the three blocks to the dark brick chapel in downtown Bear River City.

When he entered the church, sacrament meeting had already begun, and the chapel vibrated with the hearty strains of "Welcome, Welcome, Sabbath Morning."

He took a seat on the very back bench but didn't join in the singing. He was content to sit quietly and listen to the music around him. Soon, however, he found himself studying the congregation, searching. And then he found her.

Nick was sitting on the third row with her mother and brothers. She was wearing a pale blue cotton dress. Her thick, blonde hair was pulled back into an intricate French braid. She held her chin up and sang with enthusiasm. Aaron stared, admiring her pretty profile.

"I wondered if you were here," Nick greeted him as they were leaving the church three hours later, after their block of meetings. "I looked for you. I didn't see Regina and the kids either."

"I showed up late. Regina and the kids went to church with Brandon in Brigham City."

"I waited for you yesterday," Nick commented as they walked.

"Waited for *me?*"

"Hey, Coach, I run Saturdays, too."

Aaron ducked his head and rubbed the back of his neck. "Shoot! I was working on Regina's truck and forgot all about your jog."

"Actually," she admitted, "I spent the evening watching some stupid movie."

Aaron laughed. "We must have watched the same one."

"Is Regina going to be back for dinner?" Nick asked.

Aaron shook his head. "After church they were going over to one of Brandon's neighbors for dinner."

"What are your plans for dinner?"

He grinned. "I'm not really big on fasting unless there's purpose to it. I'll probably whip up a fancy peanut butter and jam sandwich, bust out a bag of potato chips, and maybe top everything off with a bowl of raspberry sherbet."

"How about coming over to our place? I think we can find something better than peanut butter sandwiches. I usually don't invite my coach to Sunday dinner. I like to keep the relationship on a professional basis, but because you look a little gaunt and your dinner prospects don't look so hot, I'll make an exception."

"Does your mom fix an extraordinary Sunday feast?"

"Oh, so you're picky? Actually, Joshua and I are fixing Sunday dinner."

"Joshua?"

Nick grinned. "Sunday dinners are a family tradition. We all take turns. There's a regular schedule. Mom is a believer that all us kids need to know how to cook—even the boys. And the ones who cook don't have to do the dishes and clean up."

"Your mom can actually get those brothers of yours to cook a Sunday dinner?"

"It would surprise you what my mother can get my brothers to do. I told you, she's the boss."

"Can anyone stand their cooking?"

"Actually, they're not too bad. They don't ever get elaborate. You know, roast, potatoes and gravy, vegetables, and a carton of ice cream."

"That's not elaborate?"

"You'll have to come sometime when Mom is cooking. Now *that's* elaborate."

"And you cook?"

"Don't act shocked."

Aaron grinned.

"Are you brave enough to try my Sunday dinner?"

"Can you cook as well as you run?"

"Better."

"Count me in. As long as Joshua is there to lend you a hand."

Thirty minutes later Aaron pulled into the Jerard driveway, parked his car in the shade of one of the big trees, and made his way to the front porch. Ruth Jerard answered the door.

"Come in, Aaron, and find yourself a place to relax," Ruth said pleasantly. "It's nice that you could come over for dinner."

Aaron walked into the living room, where four of Nick's brothers were visiting. Jared and James were each sprawled in overstuffed chairs while Joseph was stretched out on the sofa and Jacob was on the floor.

"You'll probably have to fight for a place to sit down," Ruth commented. Her sons smiled and waved at Aaron, and he returned their greeting. "Nick's in fixing dinner. She's promised her brothers that it will be ready by one-fifteen."

"And that gives you only twelve minutes," Jacob called into the kitchen from the floor.

"In twelve minutes you can start complaining," Nick called back. "And not a second before."

"I'll go give the chef a hand," Aaron grinned, backing toward the kitchen. "Need any help?" he offered. He found Nick making gravy and Joshua whipping the potatoes. She had changed out of her church clothes and was wearing a yellow dress and a blue apron. Her feet and legs were bare.

"Joshua," Nick said, "we have reinforcements. What shall we have him do?"

"He can cut up the roast. That's about the only thing left."

"Can you handle a knife without taking off a finger?"

"Mom had me work at home. She figured if we ate, we could help put the food on and take it off."

"So you're a chef, too?"

Aaron shook his head and laughed. "I didn't say I learned to cook. I just did the menial tasks. Like setting the table, clearing, and washing dishes. You know, the grubby work. Mom didn't trust me with anything very complicated. Carving a roast might be out of my league, but I'll give it a try. As long as no one complains."

"Tell that to the mob in the living room. Joshua and I won't say anything, though."

Nick walked over to him and held out a knife. "There

you go, sir. And if you don't hurry, the masses," she said, nodding toward the living room, "will get ugly."

Before the twelve minutes were up, Nick was calling her brothers and mother in to the dining area.

When the meal was over, Joshua leaned back in his chair and asked smugly, "Who are the lucky ones who get to clean up?" He grinned across the table at James and Joseph.

Aaron pushed himself to his feet and grabbed a couple of plates. "I'll lend a hand."

"But you helped with the meal," Mrs. Jerard said.

"I didn't do enough to brag about. If I had stayed home all I'd have to worry about washing would be a butter knife and a glass. But I hate eating peanut butter sandwiches and milk for Sunday dinner. After this meal, I won't be complaining about a few dishes. I insist."

"Well, if Aaron's going to play a gracious culinary saint," Nick sighed, standing up and reaching for two glasses, "I'll lend him a hand. But," she added, glaring playfully at Joseph and James, "you two'd better return the favor sometime."

"I appreciate you inviting me over," Aaron said as they worked clearing the table. "Every time I see you, I look at you from another angle. I was beginning to think you were quite the feminist."

"Oh, I'm pretty traditional. Thanks to Mom," she added, laughing.

"Your mom's quite a lady, isn't she?"

Nick was suddenly serious. "You'll never know. People think I'm so headstrong, determined, feisty—or whatever else they might think—because I have six brothers." She shook her head. "I have Mom to thank. There's nothing she would rather do than just be a mother. But things didn't work out that way for her. She said she felt so vulnerable after Dad was killed. She didn't want any of us to ever be like that, whether it was the boys in the kitchen or me out on the farm. She wanted us prepared to take care of ourselves. I love my brothers. I look up to them. But Mom's my heroine."

The two finished the dishes without saying much. Aaron dried his hands and tossed the towel to Nick. "Thanks for the dinner. I would have never guessed that a runner like you would also be a master chef."

"I usually go for a walk after dinner. It's a personal tradition. I could use some company."

"You're on. You want to change?"

Nick shook her head. "I always wear a dress on Sunday. If it can't be done in a dress, I don't do it. That's what—"

"Your mom taught you," Aaron cut in, finishing the sentence for her.

Nick smiled and nodded her head. "You're right. That's something else Mom taught me."

Aaron laughed. "Let's go for a Sunday walk. Do I need to get in my suit?"

"I would prefer that you just not put on a smart mouth."

They wandered outside, past the barn and sheds and alongside a pasture where a few cows swished flies lazily in the sun. Eventually they made their way to a dirt lane that separated a huge cornfield from an alfalfa field. Small, white butterflies fluttered about, and the buzz of bugs and bees accompanied them as they walked along side by side.

"How did things go between Regina and Brandon the other night?"

"Good, I guess. They spent all day yesterday together. They're together again today." Aaron thought a moment. "I'll have to admit one thing. Regina's been happier this past week than I've seen her for a long time."

"Tell me something. Is Regina your half sister?"

Aaron looked over at her. "No. What made you think that?"

"I just remember her telling us once that her maiden name was Tippets. You're Solinski."

Aaron glanced away. For a moment he didn't respond. When he did, he spoke in a quiet voice. "When I was nine, my dad abandoned us. He ran off with someone else. A couple years later Mom married Jack Solinski, a friend of my . . . my former father. Jack adopted me when I was a teenager. Regina was older, about to get married by then. She was never legally adopted."

"So that's why Brandon upsets you. He reminds you of your own father?" Aaron considered the question for a moment then nodded.

"Where is your dad now?" Nick asked.

"You mean Allen James Tippets?" He shrugged. "I don't know where AJ is. I know he got married a couple of times. I don't know if he's still married. Actually, I couldn't tell you for sure if the guy is alive or dead. And, frankly, I don't care."

"Aaron," she chided.

He shrugged indifferently. "I'm just stating a fact. He's been out of my life for seventeen years. If he walked up to me today, I'm not sure I'd recognize him."

The two of them walked in silence for several more minutes. "Do you regret coming to Bear River, Aaron?"

He thought a moment. Reaching down, he plucked a blade of grass and laid it in his mouth. He chewed on it and then answered, "I needed a rest." He smiled. "Sometimes I wonder if I'll be ready to give up my dump truck at the end of the summer for a pile of law books."

"You don't sound too anxious to go back to school."

"Maybe I'm not sure I want to be a lawyer right now."

"Would you rather be a truck driver?"

He shook his head. "I wouldn't mind. For a little while."

"Who's rushing you?"

"I guess myself."

Nick took a deep breath and looked up into the deep blue, cloudless sky. "If you could do anything you wanted, and you didn't have to answer to anybody, what would you do?"

Aaron rubbed the back of his neck and smiled. "Do you want to hear something dumb?"

"I'm ready for anything."

"I would like to go off to some out-of-the-way place."

"Like Bear River City?"

He shook his head and laughed. "More out-of-the-way than Bear River City. I'd like to go there—wherever that is—and teach English for a year or two. Maybe do some coaching. And just slow down."

"You don't remind me of an English teacher."

"I majored in English. I'm even certified to teach it. That was just in case I didn't get accepted to law school right away." He shook his head. "It's kind of funny, but I guess I was hoping I'd get rejected the first time around."

"Just so you could play the itinerant scholar?" She turned to look at him. "I want to teach. And coach, too. Maybe we can both find that unique little town and teach and coach. We'll be the entire faculty."

"I'm ready," he said.

"You know what I'd *really* like to do? I mean right now? Go carp fishing."

"Today?"

"Well, not on Sunday. But soon. Tomorrow."

"Why would you want to go carp fishing?"

"When I was younger I went with my brothers all the time. It's fun."

"What do you do with carp?" Aaron asked, scowling.

"Keep them. They're so huge. I think I'd love to fish for whales. You're not a fisherman?"

"Once I went to a fish hatchery. All you had to do was throw in your hook and the fish would fight each other for the privilege of getting caught. That's the extent of my fishing experience."

"That's about all the experience you need to be a carp fisherman. You can't live by the mighty Bear River for a whole summer without doing some big-time carp fishing. Let's go tomorrow."

"I guess I'm up to it. Do I need a harpoon and a peg leg?"

"No. Just a sense of adventure. And some determination. We'll see if you've got what it takes."

Chapter Eight

After work the next afternoon, Aaron and Nick climbed into Regina's '57 Chevy truck and bounced down a dirt road, through fields and groves of trees, raising a trail of gray dust behind them.

"How far are we going?" Aaron asked. "It looks like we're going away from the river."

"You don't go right to the river to catch carp. You have to go to the sloughs away from the river. Then you wade in and snatch them up."

"Wade? You didn't say anything about wading."

Nick rolled her eyes. "Does a big, tough guy like you get queasy at the thought of dipping your toe into some muddy slough water? Are you afraid you're going to melt or something? I thought someone who drives a dump truck for J. T. Overson would be able to handle a carp fishing expedition. Maybe we'd better go find a nice trout stream and a lounge chair."

"All right, all right. I was just asking. I've done a few dumb things in my life. This can't be as gut-wrenching as jumping off fifty-foot cliffs along the Salt River in Arizona."

"Probably not, but you should have worn your grubbies."

"Now you tell me," Aaron grumbled, looking down at his new Air Jordans and his hardly-been-worn Levi's.

"Carp fishing isn't exactly a gentleman's sport. But you're the one who said you wanted to go off to some

79

faraway place and play with the natives. This is the other side of your education. They don't teach you this in American Lit 590."

"Why do we need the tub?" Aaron asked, jabbing his thumb over his shoulder toward the old tin washtub that was bouncing and clanging around in the bed of the pickup.

"Some people use pitchforks to catch them." She made a face and shook her head. "I don't like to kill them. We have a pond below the house. I throw them in there."

"You have a pond stocked with carp?"

"I love going down to the pond to watch them."

Ten minutes later Aaron braked the truck to a stop at the edge of what looked like a lake with tall meadow grass and bulrushes growing around it. As he climbed from the truck, he looked out at the water and then at Nick who was beginning to open her door. "I'll get the door," he reminded her.

"You know, I'm just trying to humor you when I let you do this. But," she added with a coy smile, "I'm getting used to it."

"Keep humoring me," he said as he opened her door, bowed, and motioned with his sweeping hand for her to climb down.

"Do you do this with all the girls?"

"No, just the ones who ride in my car or truck."

"I like your sense of chivalry. But when we're done this afternoon, you're not going to feel like a gentleman or look like one."

Aaron pointed out at the water and asked, "How deep is this lake?"

"It's a slough."

"Do we need a boat? Or do we row out in the tin tub?"

"How wide do you think this is?"

"A quarter of a mile, maybe farther."

"You can walk all the way across without the water going past your knees." Nick sat down on the grass and pulled off her shoes and began to roll up her pant legs.

Aaron walked to the edge of the water and studied it more closely. "It looks kind of mucky if you ask me."

"Nobody asked you. Are you going in with your shoes on?"

"Who's idea was this?" Grumbling and shaking his head, Aaron pulled off his shoes and rolled up his Levi's.

"Grab the net," Nick called over her shoulder as she marched into the water.

Aaron picked up the net and stepped haltingly into the grayish-brown water of the slough. His feet sank into the soft ooze. "This isn't exactly a fresh water lake, is it? It's about the same temperature as leftover soup."

"That's the way the carp like it."

For the first few minutes the two waded along slowly. Then Aaron spotted a finned back sticking out of the swampy water. "There's one!" he whispered hoarsely.

"All right, get ready," Nick softly ordered. "I'll chase it to you. Get the net into the water."

"Dang, that thing's *huge!*" Aaron rasped, staring at the carp that was lazily making its way toward him. "It's got to be at least thirty inches long."

"Get ready," Nick cautioned, "I'm sending it your way."

His eyes bulging, Aaron stood with his legs apart, his body hunched over slightly and the net clutched tightly in his hands. He watched anxiously as the giant fish cruised through the water toward him. When it was about ten feet away, something spooked it, and it exploded into a writhing, twisting mass and changed direction, trying to escape.

Aaron lunged forward with his net, swooping it down into the water in the path of the fish. But then he lost his footing and was just a little off balance when the carp hit the net. The heavy fish jerked him right off his feet. He let out a shout as he plunged face first into the water.

"Don't let it get away!" Nick called out, charging forward. She splashed through the water, trying to head the carp off.

Sputtering and spitting, Aaron stood up and charged after the escaping fish. He slipped again and sprawled face down into the water as Nick tromped over him.

Gasping and gagging on the water, Aaron pushed himself up onto his knees and looked out across the water to where the carp had disappeared. "Did you see the size of that monster?" he gasped, awe-struck. "Did you see the size of it?"

Nick waved him away. "Ah, that was nothing."

"It was thirty inches long if it was a foot. It had to weigh forty pounds. I could have ridden the thing. That must have been the Moby Dick of the Bear River."

"You're all wet. And you've got mud on your face." She laughed. "And that wasn't the Moby Dick of anything. You can't really compare these to trout or bass. Carp are *big*. If you can keep from drowning in this knee-deep water, I'll show you a *big* fish."

In a few minutes they spotted another finned back slicing through the water. Aaron scrambled to get into position while Nick moved to herd it into the net. Then suddenly, out of nowhere, three other finned backs cruised toward him from another direction. Shouting and waving the net above his head, Aaron splashed blindly forward. Just before he reached the three carp, he slipped and fell headlong into the water. But in a split second he was back on his feet and sloshing wildly after the departing fish. His feet were plunging in and out of the water, his legs pumping up and down. But the fish got away. All of them.

A moment later he waded back to where Nick was impatiently standing with her hands on her hips. Aaron panted and wiped the back of his hand across his brow. "They got away," he muttered.

"I saw. The idea is to concentrate on just one fish."

Aaron nodded.

For the next forty-five minutes the two of them splashed and thrashed through the tepid waters of the slough. Before they were finished they had five carp, one of which was almost thirty-two inches long. They had filled the tin tub with water and had dumped the fish into it.

"Dang!" Aaron panted, leaning against the side of the truck and staring down into the tub filled to the brim with carp. "I've never seen anything like this. Would you just look at the size of those fish."

Nick laughed at his enthusiasm. "Don't expect to see yourself on the cover of *Field and Stream* magazine. There aren't very many people who get excited over a carp."

"You know, that's a real workout. I always thought fishing was a lazy man's sport. But this is like wrestling steers. A guy could keep in shape doing this."

"If he didn't drown first," Nick observed dryly. "I mean, this water must be all of twelve inches deep. But, we better get going if we're going to get these into the pond."

Aaron turned to get into the truck and then stopped. "Hey, we're all wet."

"We?" Nick asked, raising her eyebrows. "You got a mouse in your pocket?" She looked down at her pants. They were damp just above her knee, but she had managed to stay above water the whole while. "Not everybody wallows in the water when they go carp fishing."

"They don't?" He grinned deviously.

"I don't like that look in your eye," Nick said, beginning to back away from the pickup.

Aaron slammed the truck door and began inching

around the front of the truck. "You enjoyed letting me do all the slopping around out there, didn't you?"

Raising one hand in protest and continuing to back up, Nick called out, "Now, Aaron, I didn't make you fall down out there. I was just—"

Suddenly she turned and broke into a run, but Aaron was in close pursuit. He caught up with her before she'd taken half a dozen steps, grabbing her by the waist and stopping her flight. Then, turning Nick to face him, he held her by the wrists and began backing toward the slough, pulling her along.

"Remember, you're a gentleman," she reminded him, shaking her head and trying not to laugh. "If you'd open a door for me, you surely wouldn't—"

Before she could finish, Aaron said, "You said that when we were finished fishing, I wouldn't look or feel like a gentleman. You were right."

"Wait!" she screamed, leaning back and digging in her heels. "If we both get wet, who's going to drive?" She struggled to get free but to no avail. "You can ride in the back with the carp," she continued, "and I'll drive. Then the truck won't get wet."

"Your generosity and concern overwhelm me," Aaron came back. He lost his grip for a moment and fell backward. Nick scrambled to make her escape a second time, but Aaron caught her again before she had a chance to take a step.

Laughing and struggling, the two of them tumbled into the water and then for the next five minutes they battled each other until they were both covered with mud and water from head to foot. Finally, they dragged themselves out of the slough and collapsed in the meadow grass by the truck.

"You're a mess," Nick panted, grinning over at Aaron.

Aaron took a deep breath and stared over at Nick. Her

hair was wet and stringy and her face was streaked with mud and dirty water. Her wet clothes clung to her. "You don't look ready for the prom yourself," he grinned.

"Now, how do we drive home?"

"I've got a tarp in the truck we can throw over the seat."

"It would have been easier if you had just kept me dry."

Aaron smiled and shook his head. "The tarp will do. Besides, I'm not crazy about riding in the back of the truck with a tub full of carp."

"What happened to you?" Joseph called out as they pulled into Nick's yard a few minutes later. He looked at Aaron and Nick as they climbed out of the truck.

Jared and James soon joined Joseph. They all stared in disbelief.

"We're restocking your pond," Aaron announced, motioning them over to admire their carp catch.

The three brothers crowded around the back of the truck. "Carp?" they all said in unison.

"We got some real beauties, didn't we?" Aaron grinned.

Jared shook his head. He looked first at Nick and then at Aaron. "That's all we need. More carp."

"Did you have to get in and swim with them?" James asked.

"Only one of us got wet," Nick answered. "Then someone figured that everyone ought to get wet."

Chapter Nine

"Can you still smell carp?" Nick asked as they started their daily workout, Nick jogging and Aaron riding the ten-speed.

"Can I smell carp!" Aaron shook his head. "I soaked in the tub last night and used a quart of cologne. I don't know if it's in my head or if I still have that fishy stench hanging around me. By the way, how are Moby Dick and his friends doing?"

Nick laughed. "Moby Dick is definitely my last carp catch."

"But isn't carp fishing the main sport in Bear River City?"

She glared at him. "Do you want to get pushed off your bike?"

He grinned. "Are you going to be ready for the big race?"

"No problem."

"You aren't going to embarrass me, are you?"

"How easily do you get embarrassed?"

"Very easily."

She shrugged. "You might get embarrassed."

"What we ought to do is have you challenge a mountain. It would be good for your endurance," Aaron said.

"I don't think you could keep up." She muttered, stopping and turning to the east where three miles away the

Wasatch Mountains towered into the sky. "Do you think you could make it to the top of one of those, Coach?"

"No sweat."

"You busy Saturday?"

Aaron studied Nick for a moment. "Is that an invitation?"

She shook her head. "A challenge. Pick me up Saturday morning. You bring the drink and I'll have the lunch."

It was pleasantly cool Saturday morning as Aaron pulled into Nick's yard. The sun was just getting ready to push its way over the mountains to the east and flood the valley with golden light. He left the engine running and leaned back in his seat, waiting for Nick to come out. A chorus of birds was singing in the trees surrounding the house, and a lone cow mooed for someone to relieve her.

The screen door opened and clattered shut, and Nick came down the steps carrying a backpack bulging with a lunch. Aaron watched her approach. Her blonde hair had been gathered into a single, thick braid. She wore a long-sleeved denim shirt, a pair of faded Levi's, and brown, scuffed hiking boots. Aaron stepped from the Civic and opened the door for her.

"I hope you don't regret this hike," she commented. "It's a tough climb. It will probably embarrass you when I beat you to the top. I just hope I don't have to pack you part of the way."

"Do you always talk this much this early in the morning?" Aaron grumbled, frowning. "It should be against the law for anyone to say anything above a whisper until after six o'clock." He tried to maintain his frown, but he was laughing before he climbed in next to Nick.

The two joked and talked during the three-mile drive to Honeyville, which nestled at the foot of the mountains.

From there a dirt road wound a half mile up the mountain through sagebrush and Junegrass to where the cedar trees began to grow. Aaron parked his car in the shade of a huge maple and the two of them climbed out.

"You understand, don't you? This *is* a race," Nick announced as they were getting their things ready. "First one to the top wins."

"Is there something you know about this hike that you're not telling me, Nick? You seem too confident."

"The only thing I know is that I'm going to beat you to the top."

"I'll humor you the first nine-tenths of the way so that I'll have someone to talk to," Aaron remarked. "Then since you've made this into such a competitive thing, I'll have to leave you behind and conquer the summit alone."

When they started up the mountain, they were still in the shadows of early morning. The air was cool and refreshing, and the first half mile or so of their climb was invigorating rather than demanding. But by the time they had climbed half way up the mountain, the sun had rolled into the sky and was glaring down with an increasing intensity. The slope steepened and the vegetation thickened as they left the sagebrush and cedar trees and eventually climbed into the first pine trees.

Their conversation had been playful and joking as they started out, but gradually the talk diminished as they panted and grunted over rocks, dodged bushes and boulders, and scrambled up steeper and steeper slopes.

"You're taking this seriously, aren't you?" Aaron muttered as they rested under a pine tree and each took turns with the canteen.

"I'm going to beat you."

They pushed forward and upward, talking less and

gasping for breath more. Finally, just before ten, they spotted the summit, up past a heavy stand of pine trees.

The top was still two hundred yards away when Nick pointed and stated, "That's what we've been climbing for." Then she was off, scrambling for the lead. Aaron watched her a moment, smiling. He adjusted the pack on his back and set out after her. Although he was tired and didn't really care about being first, he kept pace with Nick until they were about fifty yards from the top. Then they broke into a gallop up the slope. They were both pulling, pushing, and shoving each other to gain an advantage.

"There's a pile of rocks up there," Nick panted. "First one there wins."

Both of them spotted the rocks at the same time. Just before they reached the rock pile Nick drove her shoulder into Aaron's side and stuck her leg out and tripped him. Her move was so unexpected and sudden that Aaron fell forward, sprawling almost spread-eagle on the ground with his pack flying in one direction and his canteen flying in another. When he looked up, Nick was standing on top of the small pile of rocks with both her hands raised above her head.

"I beat you!" she shouted in triumph.

"You cheated," Aaron countered, pushing himself to his feet and snatching up the spilled pack and canteen. "I was counting on us reaching the top together. Why does somebody always have to win?"

"You're the one who said you were going to beat me."

Wagging his head, Aaron walked the last few steps and dropped down on the ground next to the pile of rocks. Sweat was pouring down his face. His cheeks were red and his mouth was hanging open. He looked up at Nick, who was still standing above him. Her face was flushed and perspiring, but she was smiling broadly.

Nick began to survey the country around and below her, and while she wasn't watching, Aaron reached up and grasped her hand, pulling her off her triumphant perch. "Come down to earth," he teased.

"You're just jealous," she said as she regained her balance and sat down beside him.

For a moment the two of them sat in silence, gazing around them. Below was a patchwork quilt of checkered fields. The Bear River wound lazily, haphazardly below them in the valley. Towns and farms spread out in all directions.

"You know," Nick sighed, "you always wonder while you're struggling up the mountain if the effort's worth it. Once you're here and you know you've made it, once you have the view all around you, you don't question any more. You're glad you kept going."

"Especially if you beat a guy in the process," Aaron grinned, nudging her with his elbow.

She laughed. "Especially then. You hungry?"

"I've been waiting for you to ask."

"Shall we go down into the trees where it's shady?"

Aaron shook his head. "For once I'd like to eat on top of the world."

For several minutes the two munched on their sandwiches in silence, basking in the beauty of the view while a breeze blew up from the valley to cool them.

"You know, I can't figure you out, Nick."

"How's that?"

"Some girls are afraid to be too competitive with a guy." He shook his head. "Not you. You've got to prove that you can do anything a guy can do, and do it better."

She smiled and shrugged her shoulders. "Mom taught me to always do my best, regardless of the competition. Of course," she added guiltily, "she wanted me to be a lady in the process. So I humbly apologize for tripping you back there. That wasn't very ladylike of me."

"Your contrition is overwhelming, Nadine."

"What's with the *Nadine* stuff? I'll think you're my mother."

"Nadine," he said slowly as though pondering the sound. He nodded. "It fits you. Do you want to hand me another sandwich, Nadine?"

"Now don't start that," she said, blushing slightly.

"I like Nadine. Nick's too . . . too masculine. And for all of your competitiveness, you're still a lady."

"You're just sore because I beat you to the top."

"I don't get sore about things like that. I'll even let you beat me to the bottom. If you'll carry me part way down."

"Mom and my professors at USU are about the only ones who call me Nadine." She laughed softly. "I used to like Nadine and despise Nick. Now . . . " She shrugged and reached for another sandwich.

"Nadine, you're not trying out for linebacker with the Chicago Bears."

"You're beginning to sound like Jared. I think he'd like me to audition for a Betty Crocker spot."

"It's not an either-or proposition. You can push yourself to do your best and still be a lady. Didn't you tell me your mother taught you that?"

"You're not my mother, Mr. Solinski. There are a lot of things Mom can tell me that I wouldn't accept from anyone else. So don't be patronizing. Has Jared asked you to make a lady out of me?"

Aaron laughed. "I could probably do it if I put my mind to it. It would be quite a challenge, but I'd pull it off."

"I don't want to be a guy," Nick said reflectively. "I never have. That's something my brothers don't understand. They have in their mind that a girl—if she's going to be a lady—

has to run around in a dress and play in the kitchen all the time."

"And you don't agree?"

"I'm a person, not something to fit into a mold. I'm me. I like a lot of things—everything from cooking in the kitchen to hauling hay to running track." She looked over at Aaron and smiled. "To beating some guy to the top of a mountain. And none of those things have to have *boy* or *girl* written across them."

"Well, Nadine, I couldn't have said it better myself."

She glared at him. "I know. That's why I said it for you."

Smiling, Aaron finished his sandwich and leaned back, using his elbows as props. He gazed out across the valley. "I could stay here forever and just look."

Nick glanced at her watch. "I'd like to, but we'd better get going."

"What's your rush?"

Without enthusiasm she answered, "Kip Percy's picking me up at four. That won't give me a lot of time to get ready."

"I drag you all the way up here, let you see the world, and what do you do? You drop me for Kip Percy."

"I thought we came up here for training."

Aaron got to his feet, turned, and pulled Nick up. "Well, I guess the training is over," he said.

It was a few minutes after two o'clock when they finally pulled into Nick's yard. She kidded Aaron again about losing the race to the top of the mountain and before he could open the door for her, jumped out of the truck and went into the house.

Jared and Joshua were over by the barn, working together on the tractor. Aaron strolled over to say hello.

"I was hoping you'd keep her up on the mountain a couple of hours longer," Jared grinned as Aaron approached. "That way Nick would have missed Kip."

"We were on a training mission today. Training was over."

"She isn't really going to run in that 10K, is she?"

"She's not only going to run; she's going to win."

Jared eyed Aaron. "I'm not sure you're good for Nick. She'll be a confirmed jock before you're finished with her. With your fatherly influence, can't you persuade her to do something a little more feminine?"

"For example."

"Take her to dinner and a movie."

"Kip's handling that side of her. I'm training her to be a runner."

"I'd rather you took her to dinner and a movie and let Kip jog with her. Maybe he'd lose interest and go chase someone else."

"Maybe Nadine and I *will* catch a movie one of these times."

"*Nadine?*" Jared asked, amused.

"Nadine suits her."

"Don't tell her that. She'll kick you in the shin."

Aaron smiled to himself, turned, and started back for his car.

Chapter Ten

On Sunday morning Aaron managed to be in the foyer of the church when Nick came up the walk with her mother and brothers. She was wearing a navy blue suit and a white blouse. They both complemented her dark eyes and her tanned complexion. When she came through the door, she spotted him and smiled.

"You survived yesterday?" she kidded, eyeing him as though looking for some injury. She pushed against him in a playful way and nudged him with her elbow. "I thought I was going to have to drop by your sister's and drag you out of bed, Coach."

They made their way to a bench in the middle of the chapel. "Your brothers won't mind if I sit with you, will they? Regina and the kids are off with Brandon again this weekend."

She smiled and shook her head. "No, my brothers won't mind. You're family."

"The father you can't remember, is that it?"

"Oh, I think Daddy was a couple years older than you." She winked and bit down on her lip.

"What I lack in years I make up for in maturity."

Three hours later as they were leaving the building, Aaron remarked casually, "There's a fireside this evening in Brigham. You going?"

"Kip was going to pick me up." Nick took a deep breath and poked Aaron, who tried to conceal his disappointment behind a smile. "My brothers are still grumbling about the arrangement." She shook her head. "Kip and I will always be good friends. I can't seem to convince them of that."

He stopped at the end of the walk before stepping into the parking lot. Pushing his hands into his pockets, he rocked back on his heels, pressed his lips together, and glanced out across the parking lot. "Maybe another time," he said. "I'll see you tomorrow, won't I?"

"Tomorrow?"

"You're still in training, aren't you?"

She grinned and gave him a push.

"You aren't forgetting your 10K?"

"You're not serious, are you?"

"I've already signed you up and paid your ten-dollar fee. When I start coaching somebody, it's for keeps. Saturday morning at five-thirty."

"You said people shouldn't be talking before six."

"I don't want you to talk. I want you to run."

Aaron was in the living room reading when Brandon brought Regina and the kids home. They came in and started making popcorn and chocolate milk. Aaron joined them, but he was quiet amidst their laughter and banter.

Later he volunteered to put the kids to bed so that Regina and Brandon could talk. It was after ten when Brandon left.

"It's not going to be much longer, is it?" Aaron remarked as he came into the kitchen while Regina was cleaning up.

"What won't be much longer?"

"Brandon will be coming back."

Wiping the table with a wet rag, Regina remained silent. She went to the sink, washed out her rag and then answered, "Maybe not. We talked a lot about that today."

"Can you trust him?"

She thought a long while. "I suppose that's what's holding me back. We'll be together, just like before, and he'll touch me or kiss me and suddenly I go all cold inside." She swallowed and gripped the back of a kitchen chair. "And then," she whispered hoarsely, "I'll think of . . . her. And I think of him doing all of those things with her while the kids and I were . . . " She closed her eyes without finishing her sentence.

"Does Brandon know what you're thinking?"

She nodded. "It will take some time putting all of those feelings behind me. Brandon knows that. But I love him, Aaron. I've never stopped loving him. I had never seen Brandon cry until a couple of weeks ago when he asked me to forgive him, the night he took me to dinner at Maddox. He cried like a little boy. Every time we talk about what he did, he breaks up. He's really sorry."

"I still have a hard time around Brandon."

"I know. I've noticed. Brandon has noticed too. He doesn't blame you. He just wishes there were something he could do to show you that he's sincere."

"Maybe it doesn't have anything to do with Brandon. Maybe it has more to do with AJ. I think in a lot of ways Brandon personifies AJ. And I don't know that I'll ever be ready to forgive him."

"You have to forget it and go on."

"Some things I can't forget." He studied his sister as she worked at the sink. "You're not like that. When AJ left Mom, you didn't block him out. Not like me."

Regina stopped working for a moment but kept her back to her brother. "When Dad left, there wasn't anything that hurt me more. In a lot of ways Brandon's leaving wasn't as hard on me as Dad's leaving Mom and us. Maybe it has to do with how young I was. I just couldn't understand it. In a lot of ways I still can't."

"But AJ is still Dad to you."

"I still love him."

"You love AJ?"

"And feel sorry for him."

"I don't think I feel anything as kind as sorrow toward AJ," Aaron said bitterly.

"I think if you saw him and talked to him, you'd feel differently."

"I have nothing to say to him. Years ago I might have. Not any more."

"I lost contact with Daddy for several years. A few years after Brandon and I were married he wrote to me. I wrote back."

"You've written to AJ?"

"I first saw him a couple of years ago. He's different now, Aaron. You wouldn't recognize him."

"I have no desire to recognize him, meet him, or write to him or anything. He's out of my life. The same way I think Brandon ought to be out of yours."

Regina started filling the dishwasher with dirty dishes. "Did you do anything with Nick today?" she asked over her shoulder.

"Sat by her in church."

"Is anything developing there?"

Aaron laughed. "Regina, she's just a kid."

"Twenty is a kid?" She turned around.

"We're just friends. Besides, I'm family."

"There's nothing else?"

"I'm her coach, too," he joked.

"You could do worse."

"Regina, all I do is coach her a little. She dates other guys. We talk."

"Relationships have developed from much less."

* * * * *

Just before five o'clock on Saturday morning, Aaron
pulled up in his truck and touched the horn two times. A
few minutes later Nick came running out of the house wearing her sweats, munching a piece of toast and jam.

"You're early," she greeted as Aaron opened the truck
door for her.

"Early? We're barely going to make it. And why are you
eating toast?" he demanded as he closed the door behind
her.

"I'm hungry."

Aaron climbed into the truck and started out of the
driveway. "You aren't supposed to eat just before running a
10K."

"I don't have to run on an empty stomach, do I? I mean,
this is just kind of a fun jog."

"Give me the toast."

"What?"

"Give me the toast."

She handed it to him, and he tossed it out the window.

"That was the last of my breakfast."

"You're going to puke all over the course."

"I'm not either, and I hate that word. I do not *throw up*."

Aaron rolled his eyes.

"Don't worry. I'll beat most of the guys in this race."

"I hope you can beat some of the old women."

"I'll beat *all* the women, old or young."

"On a full stomach? Have you ever run a 10K? I mean
really run, for time?"

"Look, Coach," she said irritably, "you just get ready to
pick up my ribbon. This is not the first time I have run a
race. And I know what you do before a race."

"Like eat lots of toast?"

The runners were lining up when Aaron and Nick pulled up and parked the truck. Aaron raced around and helped Nick out. "Get your sweats off and start stretching," he ordered. "I'll go pick up your number and make sure your registration is straight. But hurry."

"Are you nervous?"

"I wish *you* would get nervous."

"Getting nervous wastes energy. I'm not even the coach, and I know that. I wish you hadn't thrown my toast away."

"Would you shut up and get a move on. All you've got to worry about is running this race without puking."

"Don't use that word."

"Don't you *do* it."

A few minutes later as the one hundred and twenty runners were poised at the starting line, Aaron paced anxiously to the side and shouted last-minute instructions to Nick. For the most part she ignored him, rolling her eyes occasionally without looking in his direction. The gun fired, and the crowd was off and running.

Thirty minutes later the first male runners began to return. Some minutes after that the first female, a woman in her middle twenties, burst into view and crossed the line. She was followed by a girl in her late teens and then by several other male and female runners of varying ages.

Forty-three minutes after the start of the race, Aaron spotted Nick struggling to keep a few steps ahead of a man in his middle forties. She was gasping and straining and holding her side as she stumbled over the finish line and collapsed on the grass.

Rushing over to her, Aaron grabbed her by the arm and pulled her to her feet. "You can't lie down. Keep moving."

"I can't," she groaned. "Oh, you don't know how sick I am."

"Keep moving or your muscles will cramp on you."

Although she tried to protest, Aaron dragged her by the arm and kept her moving. Sweat was pouring down her face as she continued to clutch her side and still suck in huge gulps of air.

"I feel sick," she moaned.

Aaron looked over at her, disgusted. Her face had turned a sickly gray. She began to shake her head. "I think I'm going to throw up," she groaned. "I've got to get someplace where—"

She didn't finish her sentence. Suddenly she bent over and retched. Aaron rolled his eyes and shook his head. Several people were close by and saw it all. She retched again.

"Well, at least you puked in the dirt and not on the road," Aaron grumbled. "That makes a terrible mess on the pavement. Everybody tromping through it."

For another moment she was motionless, hunched over with her hands on her knees and her head hanging down. She gagged and spit. Slowly she straightened up and noticed Aaron watching her.

"Do you have to watch me do this?" she snapped weakly.

"Believe me, this isn't any more appetizing for me than it is for you. Do you think I want to see you or anybody else pu— excuse me, throw up? What did you have for breakfast anyway?"

"A couple of eggs, some juice, and toast."

"Before a 10K?"

"I've never had to worry about eating breakfast."

"And here I thought you were a seasoned—"

"Just shut up."

He tossed a towel to her so she could wipe her face. "Can you make it back to the truck?"

She nodded.

"I don't know how to break this to you," Aaron

commented as they were driving home a few minutes later, "but I had to leave your ribbon back there."

"Are you going to rub it in?" She leaned her head out the window slightly so that the air could wash over her.

Aaron smiled. "A few of the girls beat you in."

"I started out too fast." She swallowed painfully. "But I didn't stop running once," she added in her defense.

"Maybe you should have stopped sooner."

"I'm no quitter. I told myself as soon as my side started hurting that I would die before I stopped."

"The first woman finished in just under thirty-eight minutes."

"What did I do?"

"Forty-two, thirty-seven."

"I could do it lots faster than that."

"Not with your belly full of breakfast."

"I wish you hadn't seen me throw up."

Aaron laughed. "I wish I had seen you win. Whether you puke after that doesn't make any difference to me. I've seen lots of people puke."

"You haven't seen me. Nobody has seen me do that."

Aaron wagged his head and grinned. "What an honor. I'm the only guy who has ever seen Nadine Jerard puke."

"Would you shut up?"

"I have had the unique privilege of watching you—"

"Aaron," she cut in, turning on him, "if you say one more word about that I'm going to kick you right out of that door. And I hope the truck runs over you."

He held up a hand in a gesture of peace. "I won't say another word."

"And I don't want you to tell my brothers anything."

"They haven't seen you either?"

She glowered over at him. He didn't say anything more until he pulled into her yard. As he was helping her out of the truck, he remarked, "What happened today is between you and me. On one condition."

"What's that?"

"You run again Saturday."

"Saturday?"

"This time you run against the clock. No spectators, no cheers, no fanfare, no nothing. Just a long, hard race. But you do it on an empty stomach. I think you can beat that other woman's time. There isn't any ribbon or glory in it. This is just to humor me, to prove to me that I'm not coaching a pukin' little girl."

She glared at him for a moment and then nodded her head once. "But you realize the 10K isn't my race."

"It is next Saturday. You've got to beat thirty-eight minutes. And that's no slow walk."

The rest of the day Aaron puttered about his sister's place working on the Chevy, but the whole while he felt empty. Midafternoon he climbed into the truck and drove around. At first he told himself that he was just seeing how the old truck ran, but eventually he ended up at Nick's place.

"How're things going?" Joshua called to Aaron as he pulled up and climbed from the truck. Joshua was at the corral working on one of the gates.

Aaron strolled over and gave him a hand. They worked in silence for a moment and then Joshua grunted as he pulled a wire tight, "How'd Nick do this morning in her race?"

"She did all right," he answered. "Inexperience was her biggest enemy. She's coming along."

"It wiped her out. She came home and went straight to bed. Wouldn't say a word about what happened."

"Is she all right?"

Joshua nodded. "She got up a few minutes ago. I think she's in the backyard."

"Maybe I'll wander around that way."

Aaron spotted her as he walked around the back corner of the house. She was wearing blue jeans and an oversized T-shirt and was sitting in a lawn chair under a big tree. Her feet were bare, and her legs were pulled up in front of her. She had her arms wrapped around them and was resting her cheek on her knees. Her hair was loose and hung down, partially hiding her face.

For a moment Aaron stood at the corner of the house and looked. After a moment, he approached slowly, walking quietly across the grass. When he reached her, he sat down in a chair next to hers without making any noise. "How do you feel?" he asked gently. Her eyes opened suddenly and she straightened up. "How's the road racer?"

"Don't start rubbing anything—"

Aaron reached out suddenly and put his hand on her mouth. "I'm not going to hassle you. I just dropped by to check up on you. What's a coach for?"

Nick put her legs down and stretched. "I feel dumb, if you want to know the truth."

"What are you doing tonight?"

"Nothing."

"How would you like to do something?"

"What did you have in mind?"

Aaron shrugged. "Oh, something fun and exciting. Bear River City is getting a little slow for me. And the coach needs to get to know his pupil better."

"So you just want to coach me some more?"

He laughed and shook his head. "No coaching. Honest."

"There's a rodeo at the county fairgrounds arena," she suggested.

"I've never been to a rodeo."

Nick pulled the corners of her mouth down and cocked her head to one side. "You're from Arizona and haven't ever seen a rodeo?"

"Do you go to rodeos much?" he asked.

"I used to go with my brothers all the time. It's been a while since they've taken me."

"Will your brothers trust you with me at a rodeo?"

She laughed. "I think so. You're like another big brother."

Aaron glanced over at her. "Well, that's the first time I've ever asked a girl to do something and she's accused me of being just like her big brother."

"Are you serious about going to the rodeo?"

Aaron pushed himself to his feet. "You just get into your boots and chaps, and I'll be here."

Chapter Eleven

"No boots, no jeans, no cowboy hat?" Nick greeted
Aaron as she opened the front door for him and saw him
dressed in a pair of slacks, a pull-over knit shirt, and a pair of
penny loafers. "When you go to a rodeo, you should dress
the part."

Aaron smiled and stared at Nick, who was wearing a
pair of Wrangler jeans; a blue, western-style shirt; and soft
leather, tan cowboy boots. Her straw Stetson sat prettily on
her head.

"I didn't know I was going with Annie Oakley. You
dressed up enough for both of us."

Jared came up behind Nick and looked over her shoulder at Aaron. "Can you take care of her at a rodeo?" he
asked with a grin. "Sometimes she gets pretty excited. Keep
a tight rein on her."

The rodeo was new to Aaron, but having Nick there
made it interesting. She was excited the whole time, standing up and shouting and explaining everything the riders
and ropers did, right and wrong, even before the judges had
a chance to announce their decisions.

"You really get into this rodeo thing, don't you?" Aaron
kidded as Nick bounced up and down on the bench during
the bareback riding.

Blushing, she laughed. "I think that's why my brothers

stopped bringing me. They thought I got too wild. Am I embarrassing you?"

"Not yet. Most everybody just assumes you're my kid sister, and they seem pretty understanding."

"I thought most of them assumed you were my dad."

"Don't get smart."

When the bull riding started, Nick leaned over and said, "Todd Macey should win this one."

Aaron glanced over at her. "*Our* Todd Macey?"

She nodded. "For all he's not, he is great on a bull."

The first few bull riders were mediocre, and then the announcer called Todd Macey's name. When the gate burst open, a huge Brahma lunged out—a twisting, writhing, kicking mass of pent-up rage, but Todd held on like a persistent burr, waving one hand high above his head while gripping the sides of the bull tightly with his legs. The bull seemed to go in five directions at once, but Todd never lost his grip until the horn sounded. Then he let go of the surcingle and jumped clear as the bull bucked out from under him. He landed on his feet and strutted back toward the chutes, his chaps flapping as he walked.

Even Aaron, who didn't know anything about bull riding, could tell that Todd had outshined the previous riders. "He's good, isn't he?" Nick said enthusiastically.

"I'm just glad it's him riding the bulls and not me."

When the rodeo was over, they made their way from the stands and pushed through the crowd to the parking area behind the chutes and corrals. They passed a number of horse trailers where cowboys were milling around, talking and laughing. Nick seemed to know many of them.

"Hey, Roger," Nick called out to a cowboy lugging a saddle to a bale of straw. "That was a good ride."

The cowboy grinned and waved.

"Great roping, Travis," she called to another.

As they walked along, several of the cowboys joked with Nick. "You're right at home here," Aaron laughed.

"They're friends."

"Have you ever wanted to join the rodeo?"

She shook her head. "It's a pretty rough life. I like watching it from the stands, but I'm always a little disappointed when I come back this way and see the other side of it. Back here you see the chewing and smoking and smell the booze. It's not as exciting close up."

"Hey, Nick." Aaron and Nick stopped and glanced toward a group of cowboys lounging about the tailgate of a horse trailer. Several of them were each holding a can of beer. Todd Macey, leaning against the horse trailer, waved. His shirt was unbuttoned with the tails hanging out. Nick smiled thinly when she recognized him. "You haven't lost your touch, Todd," she said. "You better start packing for the Nationals."

Todd shrugged in an attempt to appear modest, but his cockiness prevailed. "Thanks," he gloated. He glanced at Aaron. "I haven't seen you around much, Nick."

"It gets that way in the summer. Too much going on." She saw how he was looking at Aaron, and it made her nervous. Anxiously she reached out and took Aaron's hand and started moving away.

"Some of us guys were going to get something to eat in a bit. Come along. I'll buy."

Nick smiled and shook her head. "Thanks, but we've got to be going."

"You can drag along your dude friend." Todd stood and folded his arms across his chest.

Aaron smiled and shook his head. "Thanks, Todd, but we had other plans. It was a good ride. I was impressed."

"Maybe Nick wants to stay, Dude," Todd commented, taking a couple of steps toward them.

Aaron smiled. "I doubt it." He and Nick started walking away.

"You and me still have a score to settle, Dude." Aaron stopped with his back to Todd Macey. Todd laughed sardonically. "But I'll let you tuck your tail and run one more time. Because you're with Nick."

Aaron turned around. He forced out a hoarse laugh and began to rub the back of his neck with his hand, looking down at the ground. Poking the toe of his shoe into the gravel, he answered, "As I remember it, Cowboy, when you're not falling all over yourself, you're the one who tucks tail and runs."

Todd bristled, but he forced himself to continue smiling.

"Aaron, let's go," Nick rasped, taking Aaron's hand and tugging anxiously.

"You better go with the little lady tonight, Dude. But I can wait. I've got lots of time."

Nick turned on Todd. "Let it alone," she bristled. "The other night wasn't Aaron's fault. He was just trying to help out."

"Next time he better not poke his nose into my business."

Nick took a couple of steps toward Todd. "Don't you ever get tired of playing the tough guy?" she snapped.

Two cowboys stepped forward and each took Nick by an arm and pulled her to the side. She tried to shake herself free, but the two held her. "Todd, stop it!" she called out angrily as Todd grinned toward Aaron. "Leave him alone, Todd."

"She's pretty protective of you, Dude. Too bad her brothers aren't around to rescue you."

"Tell your two friends to take their hands off Nick. We were just passing through to get to the car. We don't have anything to say to you or your friends."

Todd laughed and stuffed his hands into his rear pants pockets. "Oh, we're touchy tonight. You're not nervous, are you?" He laughed again. "It's just you and me, Dude."

Aaron stared back for a moment without changing his stony expression. "Tell your two friends to let Nick go," he ordered huskily.

"They're just watching out for her."

The muscles along Aaron's jaw tightened and he swallowed away the dryness in his throat. "You should have stuck to riding bulls, Macey, where you've always got a clown around to pull you out of trouble."

The challenging smile on Todd's face disappeared. "Some things I do better than ride bulls, Dude."

"Like move your mouth?"

Todd Macey hesitated only a moment and then suddenly lunged toward Aaron. Nick screamed as Todd threw a wild punch at Aaron. Aaron rocked back and ducked, avoiding the viscious blow. At the same moment he stepped back, his left fist flashed forward and caught Todd full in the face. The punch was so quick and unexpected that it brought Todd up short. He staggered backward, shaking his head slightly and touching his hand to his nose. He brought his hand away bloody.

"All right, Dude, you're mine," Todd growled. He charged again, this time his fists up, his body hunched slightly.

Aaron took a couple of steps backward. He brought his fists up and began to dance on the balls of his feet, his eyes riveted to Todd. As Todd moved in, Aaron danced just out of reach and then moved forward with a short, hard left jab leading the way. Three times his left fist fired out, banging each time into Todd's face. Todd lashed out with his fists, but he only punched thin air. Then Aaron methodically came across with a mean right punch that snapped Todd's head back. Aaron threw two quick punches to Todd's exposed midsection and then sent another punishing fist to the side of his jaw, sending him sprawling in the gravel and dirt.

Everyone who had suddenly gathered to watch stared in silent disbelief. Slowly Todd stirred, rolled over on his stomach, and pushed himself up on his hands and knees. He looked dumbly up at Aaron, who was standing calmly a few feet away rubbing and massaging his knuckles. "You're a better bull rider, Macey."

Aaron stepped over to where Nick stood between the two cowboys. She gaped in mute horror, first at Todd and then at Aaron.

One of the two cowboys released his grip on Nick's arm. The other one refused momentarily. "I'm not in the mood to ask twice, Cowboy," Aaron warned.

Slowly the cowboy released his hold on Nick's arm and took a short step away from her. Aaron took Nick by the hand and started away from Todd Macey and his group. Nick and Aaron didn't speak until they were in the car.

"I wish you hadn't seen that," Aaron said, speaking first.

"I guess I understand now why you didn't want Jared and Joshua's help the other night." She stared straight ahead. "That wasn't your first fight, was it?"

"If it had been my first one, I would be back there right now spitting blood and picking my teeth out of the gravel."

She didn't answer.

"Macey was the one pushing for the fight."

"I know."

"Are you upset with me?"

"Surprised. Maybe a little disappointed."

"Because I defended myself?"

"It was the way you did it. It was so brutal. So coldly professional."

"There's no pretty way to fight, Nick."

"I wasn't expecting that from you."

"Nick, I don't go around picking fights. I didn't pick this one tonight. I tried to walk away from it. But once it started, I had to defend myself."

"Where did you learn to do that?"

"Mostly from my father. He was a semiprofessional boxer when he was younger. He taught me what to do in a jam. Most of the fighting I've done has been in a gym. That's the first fight I've been in since high school. I doubt your friend Todd could say the same."

"I'm not worried about Todd."

Aaron heaved a sigh. "Do you want to get something to eat?"

"I'd like to go home."

Neither of them spoke as they drove to Nick's house. When they pulled into the yard, Aaron parked the car, got out, and opened the door for Nick. "I'm sorry about tonight," Aaron apologized. "I had hoped for a better ending to the evening."

Nick avoided his gaze, choosing instead to stare blankly at the light burning on the porch. "I know it wasn't your fault," she said softly. "Good night."

Aaron was depressed and discouraged as he entered his sister's house a few minutes later. Regina was still up, sitting on the living room sofa writing a letter.

"What's the matter?" she asked, looking up as Aaron walked into the room.

Aaron stuffed his hands into his pockets and stood in the middle of the room. "Let's just say that I had hoped things would work out a little better."

"What happened?"

"I got into a fight."

"With Nick?"

"With Todd Macey."

"Oh." She put her writing tablet beside her. "You don't look any worse for wear."

He pulled his hands from his pockets and stared down at them. "I busted open two of my knuckles. For a while I thought I'd broken my hand, but I think it's just bruised." Stuffing his fists back into his pockets, he commented, "I don't think Nick was at all impressed." He smiled. "I guess I should have stuck to coaching."

"You like her, don't you?"

"She's a good kid."

"I know. But you like her, too. And not as just a good kid."

"Regina," he stopped her, "Nick and I are friends. At least we were. It's hard to know what will happen after tonight."

Chapter Twelve

Monday evening Nick was jogging along the county road, hoping to rid herself of some of the tension and frustration she had been battling over the past two days. She was on the bridge before she noticed Aaron waiting for her. He was standing there next to the ten-speed, dressed in a pair of sweatpants and a T-shirt, with his arms folded across his chest, staring out across the river.

Fifteen or twenty feet from him Nick slowed to a walk and then stopped altogether, breathing heavily. Aaron glanced down at his watch and then looked at her for the first time. "You're late. I got to wondering if you were going to show."

Nick didn't respond.

"I've charted out your 10K course. We'll start at your place at five-thirty Saturday morning. Remember, you've got to do it in under thirty-eight minutes."

Nick started running. A moment later Aaron had caught up to her, riding beside her on the bike. For the rest of Nick's jog, neither of them spoke. They crossed the bridge again and then headed for Nick's place. As they reached the driveway, she slowed to a walk, and Aaron climbed off his bike and pushed it along beside her.

"I was going to Cedar City this weekend to visit my folks," Aaron commented. "But I canceled out. Because of the big race. Had you run up to standard last Saturday, I could have gone."

"You should still go."

He shook his head. "I never abandon a struggling pupil. You'll never know if you can run a 10K in under thirty-eight minutes if I don't push you."

"What makes you think I'm even going to run?"

"Pride."

"Yours or mine?"

Aaron smiled. "Both." He wiped his brow with the back of his hand. "Still simmering because of Saturday night?"

"You better go visit your parents."

He smiled. "I can't. I'm working late Friday evening. I had hoped I'd have all day Friday off." He shook his head. "We're behind, though. You're really not messing up my plans."

For the rest of the week Aaron met Nick at the bridge like he had always done. Nick remained cool but responded to his coaching suggestions, pushing herself more, sprinting the last quarter mile, concentrating on picking up her feet.

"Now don't tank up this time," Aaron cautioned as they finished their workout Friday evening. "Get some liquid in you tonight. Don't eat anything heavy. And get a good night's sleep."

"Kip's taking me out tonight."

Aaron squeezed the front bike tire, checking the air. "Tell him to get you in early," he ordered matter-of-factly.

"You don't give up, do you?"

Aaron smiled and shook his head. "Once I set my mind to something, I go after it. I want to see you run a 10K under thirty-eight minutes. I want to know if I figured you wrong."

"Like I figured you wrong?"

He stared at her for a moment without answering. "I'll

be here at five-thirty in the morning." He pursed his lips pensively, climbed onto his bike, and pushed away.

As Aaron drove up the following morning in his sister's truck, he spotted Nick stretching and massaging her leg muscles.

"You're up," he commented in greeting as he walked up. "I wasn't sure you'd follow through."

She glanced at him. "I have something to prove to myself."

"Your stomach empty?"

She nodded.

"Get a good sleep?"

"I was in at eleven-fifteen."

He permitted himself a smile.

Pushing herself to her feet, she started jogging slowly toward the road. "Where does the course start?"

Aaron returned to the truck and pulled the ten-speed out of the back. He pushed it to the lane where Nick was waiting for him.

"We start at the corner of the cornfield. You'll run to the river, cross the bridge, and head for town. Go to the church, turn left onto the main highway, go down three blocks, turn left and then you head back this way. You'll fin-ish here."

She stared at his bike. "You figure you have to chase me all the way?"

"I'm going to pace you."

The two went to the starting area. Nick was gently shak-ing her hands and arms and jogging in place on her toes. Aaron readied his stopwatch and glanced over at Nick, who was now set. "You ready?" She nodded once, staring intently at the road ahead, her body tense and waiting. "Go for it,"

Aaron called out, punching the stopwatch and pushing off on his bike.

They both moved down the road, neither speaking for the first mile. When they spotted the river, Aaron glanced at his watch and remarked, "Pick it up a little."

Nick's breathing was steady and deep, but in the cool of the morning she still hadn't broken into a sweat. They dropped into the river bottom and crossed the bridge. "Take it easy as you're going up the hill out of the bottom," Aaron cautioned. "You can make up time on the level stretches."

When they reached the church and started down the highway, Nick's breathing was deeper, heavier, but she wasn't slowing down. When they turned and doubled back past the church and headed for home, Aaron studied his watch a moment and then prodded, "You've got to pick it up. Push it. You can't drag now."

They left the church behind them and headed back toward the river. Nick was red-faced and straining, breathing heavily, but she had her second wind. As they climbed out of the river bottom and entered the last straight stretch, Aaron called over to her, "A little over a mile to go. This is where you win. Pick up your feet and really push it. This is the reason you did all the windsprints." He paused a moment and then added as an afterthought, "And whatever you do, don't puke yet."

Her eyes turned on him irritably for a moment, but she didn't speak.

A quarter mile from the finish line, Aaron passed her on the bike and sped to the end of the course. He climbed off and stood at the finish line. "Come on, Nadine," he shouted down the road. "Sprint. Give it everything you've got."

She quickened her pace, but she was hurting. The pain,

however, didn't deter her. She began to sprint and when she crossed the finish line, she was gasping and groaning.

For the next several minutes she walked to keep the stiffness out of her legs and to catch her breath. When she finally returned to where Aaron waited for her at the finish line, she was holding her side and grimacing.

"How did I do?" she demanded hoarsely.

"You didn't break any world record."

She swallowed and wet her lips. "I gave it all I had."

"Well, at least you didn't puke."

"How fast did I run?" she snapped angrily.

Aaron walked over to the bike, picked it up, and began pushing it to the truck.

"How fast?"

Aaron stopped and turned around. "Thirty-seven, fifty-two," he said, suddenly smiling.

She stared a moment as though not hearing and then a grin crinkled her features as she took another deep breath. "I did it," she murmured.

"I don't expect you to thank me, even though I did push you the whole way."

"Thanks," she laughed.

"Don't celebrate yet. I don't even know if thirty-seven, fifty-two is any good for a 10K."

Her grin drooped momentarily.

"But," he added, "it would have won you the race last weekend."

The grin returned. "I'm going to make the USU track team," she said with confidence.

"You'll need a coach."

"I thought I had one."

"I'm not sure I can handle someone who's so moody."

She looked down.

"We really ought to celebrate. Nothing big. We could go

get a hamburger or something. I'll pick you up this evening at seven."

Nick stared at him with a pained expression. "Kip kind of asked me to go with him to a family picnic."

"He kind of asked?"

"He asked. I just didn't give him a real firm answer."

"Then just give him a firm no."

She smiled and then nodded.

"You look happy," Joshua remarked to Nick that evening as she came out of the bathroom in her robe with a towel wrapped around her head. "You've been whistling and singing ever since you climbed into the shower. Where you headed tonight?"

"To celebrate," she said, stopping in the hall and turning to face her brother.

"Celebrate what?"

"I ran the 10K in under thirty-eight minutes."

"Is that good?"

She pulled the towel off her head and began massaging her hair vigorously with it. "I don't know," she answered. "It's better than I've done."

"And who are you celebrating with?"

"Aaron's taking me out for a hamburger or something."

"I thought you were finished with him after his fight with Todd Macey."

She straightened up, shook her wet hair a bit, and tossed the towel over her shoulder. She shrugged, opening her door.

"Do you like this guy?" Joshua questioned.

Nick dropped down on the edge of the bed and looked at her brother, who was leaning in the doorway. "He's my coach," she answered, laughing.

Joshua thought for a moment and then smiled. "You sure

wouldn't have to worry about a bodyguard." He snorted. "Every time I think of Jared and me trying to defend him at that young adult party, I get a good laugh. He could have probably taken all three of us on." He became serious. "You like him, don't you?"

"Joshua, I didn't say I liked him."

Joshua pushed away from the door jamb. "You didn't have to."

Nick was waiting on the lawn when Aaron pulled up just after seven. She walked out to the Civic as he climbed from the car.

"You look a little fresher than you did this morning," Aaron greeted her as he looked at the white slacks and pink blouse she was wearing. "I think it's the smile," he commented as he helped her into the car and closed the door. "I didn't ever picture you wearing anything pink."

She laughed and shook her head. "Since I'm Nadine to you," she said dubiously, "and since Nadine is kinda pinkish, I thought I'd wear it. It's the only pink thing I own. Jared bought it for me a couple years ago. I have to wear it occasionally to show my appreciation."

He studied her a moment and then nodded his head. "It does make you look like a genuine Nadine."

"I'm not sure that's a compliment."

"Definitely a compliment." He started driving down the road. "Ever since coming here, everyone has told me about this real hot spot in Brigham. A drive-in called Peach City."

She laughed. "The ultimate stop."

"Is it true that they still have carhops?"

She nodded.

"I thought carhops and drive-ins were chased out by McDonald's and Taco Bell."

"Not at Peach City." She smiled. "I always wanted to be

a carhop at Peach City." She looked over at him. "All the girls wanted to work there. The guys were always pulling in and checking them out."

"Why didn't you go for it?"

"It was either play ball and study or work at Peach City. Ball and books won out."

"Is the food edible?"

"Can't beat it."

"Better than Burger King?"

"Not even close."

"Then we're off to Peach City."

The parking lot at Peach City was packed. The carhops were rushing in and out of the drive-in, taking orders, carrying out trays heaped with hamburgers, fries, drinks, and shakes.

"It's bigger than I thought it would be," Aaron commented, studying the place. "Is there a place inside where we can eat?"

Nick nodded.

"Let's go in there."

They climbed from the Civic and headed across the busy parking lot. "Looks like this is where everybody comes for excitement on a Saturday night."

They stepped inside the dining area, and the door closed behind them. There was one vacant booth against the back wall. They both spotted it at the same time. But they also saw who was in the next booth—Todd Macey and two of his friends!

"Let's eat in the car," Nick rasped, squeezing Aaron's hand.

Gently but firmly Aaron pulled his hand from Nick's grasp and started toward the empty booth. Nick followed reluctantly.

Todd saw them as they approached. Up until then the

two guys he was with had been laughing and talking. But when Todd saw Aaron and Nick, the talking stopped.

Aaron nodded a silent greeting to Todd, who stared motionless. Traces of last week's fight still lingered on Todd's face—a blackish-blue right eye and a puffy, yellowish bruise on his left cheek.

Nick stood stiffly, her face taut and tense, her eyes wide and staring. Aaron nudged her and helped her into the empty booth.

"That was close," she whispered across the table when they were both seated.

Aaron propped his elbows on the table and let his chin rest lightly on the tips of his fingers. He stared across the table at Nick, and a smile twitched at the corners of his mouth. "I'll be right back."

Aaron slid out of the booth and turned to Todd and his two friends. He sat down across the table from Todd. "Can I sit down?"

Todd glared. "Looks like you're already down."

"How's the eye?"

"What do you want?"

"No hard feelings."

"Get real, Dude."

Aaron shrugged. "I'm sorry about the other night. I wasn't looking for a fight. But I don't make it a habit of letting guys punch my lights out, either. You kind of pushed me into a corner."

Todd stared across the table. "What do you want?"

Slowly and unexpectedly, Aaron extended his hand. "I'm sorry. Can we forget it?"

Todd stared across the table at the outstretched hand without taking it. Finally Aaron withdrew his hand and stood up. "I didn't have anything against you the other night, Todd. I still don't."

Turning, he returned to his own booth, where Nick had sat, watching. Todd and his two friends pushed out of their booth. As they walked past Nick and Aaron toward the door, they stared straight ahead.

"What was that about?" Nick rasped.

"I'm not Christian enough to turn my cheek to someone like Todd Macey, but I don't like to stay angry with someone for long either."

"It didn't look like Todd shared your Christian spirit."

For a long time the two sat there, staring down at the table without speaking. Finally Aaron heaved a sigh and remarked, "Well, I'm never going to know if Peach City burgers are as good as everyone says unless we order."

"I'm not sure I understand you, Aaron."

"I'm not sure I understand myself."

A summer shower had soaked and freshened the countryside. The black road glistened from the recent rain as they approached the river. "Stop on the bridge," Nick called out. "Look at that gorgeous full moon peeking out from the hole in the clouds."

Aaron pulled the car to the side of the road, and the two of them strolled onto the bridge. For a moment they leaned their forearms on the cable guardrails and enjoyed looking at the shimmering reflection of the moon on the ebony waters, listening to the lap of the water against the pilings below.

"It's been almost a month now," Nick commented.

"Since what?"

"Since we've known each other. The moon was full the first time we crossed here at night."

Aaron nodded, feeling a warm longing. He stared at Nick in the darkness. With the moon as bright as it was, he could see her face clearly. "What are you doing Friday night?" Before she could answer, he quickly added, "Tell him you can't." She looked over at him. "Friday's reserved," he said simply.

"Where are we going?"

"As far as we can get from any rodeo or hamburger joint. I'm taking you to the Brass Stag. We'll have dinner and go dancing."

"Is that a polite way of telling me not to wear my boots and jeans?"

Aaron pushed away from the bridge and looked at Nick.

"You sure you want to blow everything on the Brass Stag?"

"Not on the Brass Stag. On you."

Ruth Jerard stopped by Nick's room that night. "Is there anything between you and Aaron?" she asked.

Nick rolled her eyes. "Mother, we went for a hamburger. He made me run a race today."

Mrs. Jerard held up her hands. "I was just wondering."

"We're friends. Good friends."

Mrs. Jerard smiled. "You could do worse, you know."

"Mom, Aaron is like a brother. Not so much of a tease, though. Besides, he's a lot older than I am."

"Your father was four years older than I."

"Aaron's Jeremiah's age, *seven years older* than I am. I was in sixth grade when he left to go on his mission."

"You're not in sixth grade anymore." Mrs. Jerard smiled.

"I haven't even had a real date with him."

"Tonight wasn't a real date?" Mrs. Jerard asked, lifting her eyebrows.

"Not really. But he asked me to go out with him next Friday night. He said he wants to take me to dinner at the Brass Stag in Salt Lake."

"Well! *That* sounds like a real date. Your father and I

went there once for our anniversary. It's a very fancy place. What will you wear?"

"I don't know. What *do* you wear to a place like that?"

"You'll want to dress up. It sounds like we may need to do some shopping."

Nick looked at her mother. "Maybe I do like him in a different way than I do the boys." She shrugged. "Maybe I like him a little bit."

"Are you ready to get serious?"

"Mom, I just like running around with him. Literally."

"Just remember to use your head as well as your heart, Nadine."

"Mother!"

She held up her hands. "I'm just passing out a little advice. Mothers have a right to do that, you know. Even when their daughters think they're all grown up."

Nick laughed and shook her head. "Thanks, Mom. I'll have to admit that most of your counsel has been good so far."

"Just most of it?" She raised her brows teasingly. "I thought it was all good." She started for the door but paused in the doorway and turned around. "I know it might not make a lot of difference to you, but I like Aaron. I liked him the first time I met him."

"Thanks, Mom. That means a lot."

Chapter Thirteen

"He just drove in," Joshua called down the hall to his sister.

"I'll be there in a second," she gasped as she rushed from her bedroom to the bathroom down the hall. She had already put her makeup on but was still wearing a bathrobe.

"You're not nervous are you?" Joshua kidded, stepping to the open bathroom door to watch Nick evaluate herself in the mirror above the sink.

"Do I look all right?"

"Nick, it's just Aaron. I mean, he's seen you every which way. Everything from cowboy boots to jogging suit. Why get nervous all of a sudden?"

"You're no help at all," she snapped.

When Aaron knocked on the front door, Nick's five unmarried brothers were waiting in the living room. He stepped inside wearing a blue blazer, white shirt and tie, and dark pants. He was holding a box of flowers in his hand.

"This *is* fancy stuff," Jared joked as he motioned Aaron toward the living room sofa with a jerk of his head.

Aaron's face glowed red under his dark tan. "Sometimes a guy has to splurge a little."

"The Brass Stag is just a little splurging?" Jared came back. "Isn't that the place on the east side of Salt Lake?"

Aaron shrugged. "I hear it's a notch or two above Taco Bell."

"I've never seen Nick quite so nervous," Joshua commented, dropping onto the love seat and winking at his brothers. "What did you tell her about tonight?" he asked Aaron.

"Not to get nervous."

Nick and her mom had gone shopping at the Bon Marche in Ogden one night after work. They had debated over several dresses and outfits. What they had finally purchased seemed to work. As Nick came quietly into the living room, all eyes turned in her direction and six mouths dropped open. Mrs. Jerard followed her daughter into the room and stood to one side, smiling proudly.

Nick was wearing a pair of high-waisted, black slacks and a silky, long-sleeved, cream-colored blouse. She had on a pair of black patent leather, medium high heels and had pulled her hair back into an intricate French braid. The golden earrings she wore caught the light and framed her face. It was a simple but elegant look. She was beautiful.

"Hello," Aaron greeted somewhat stunned, pushing up from the sofa and fidgeting a moment. He studied her and then glanced down at the box in his hands.

"You didn't have to do that," Nick answered, her cheeks coloring as she took the flowers.

"She's definitely not going to run a 10K tonight," Jared teased, grinning at his brothers.

"Would you boys go on about your business," Ruth Jerard ordered. "Hello, Aaron," she greeted, shaking Aaron's hand. "You two look like you're ready for a big night."

"Now, Mom, don't you start. Can you help me with these flowers? They're beautiful."

"After I herd your brothers out of here. Now you boys get!" She tried to sound stern but her smile diluted the effect. The boys shuffled reluctantly out of the room, and Mrs. Jerard went to find a vase.

* * * * *

As the front door closed behind Nick and Aaron, the brothers returned to the living room, where Mrs. Jerard was still fussing with the arrangement of flowers.

Joshua remarked, "Something tells me those two stopped being just friends."

"Where did Nick get that outfit?" Jared asked, scratching his head. "She'll have everybody in the country looking at her."

"For your information, Jared," his mother said, "the boys have been noticing Nadine for a good long while. Aaron isn't the first. But I think he's the first that Nadine has responded to with so much interest."

"I hope she doesn't forget Richard Robbins is going to be home before long," Jared remarked seriously.

"He better get here pretty soon," James spoke out, "or Nick isn't even going to be around."

"Why don't you boys let Nadine worry about her social life."

"You don't think she should wait for Richard?" Jared wanted to know.

"Only if she wants to."

The night was beginning to cool as Nick and Aaron stepped off the porch and strolled toward Regina's Chevy truck. "When I told you we were going fancy," Aaron apologized, "that didn't include transportation. The Civic is being tempermental again. Besides," he shrugged, smiling, "I kinda like the old Chevy. It's classy in its own way. I even cleaned it out and washed it down."

"I have fond memories of the Chevy. Regina used to take us Laurels for rides."

Aaron hesitated before opening the truck door for her. "You look nice tonight, Nadine." He smiled.

As Nick climbed into the truck she sat on the passenger side. When Aaron climbed in, he glanced over at her and grinned, "If you sit way over there, I'll have to shout just to carry on a conversation."

Blushing, she moved halfway over. "It feels a little strange after being . . ." She paused and her blush deepened.

Reaching over, Aaron took her by the hand and tugged gently. "I need someone to shift the gears." She slid next to him and operated the gear shift.

There was a trace of tension as they started out, but by the time they had reached the freeway on-ramp just west of Honeyville, their nervousness had dissipated.

"Does everyone who takes you out get the same high-powered reception? I mean from the fraternal honor guard back there."

Nick laughed and shook her head. "The boys are there mostly to tease. They know they can be intimidating. They do it mainly to embarrass me." She looked over at him. "Did you mind?"

"I would probably have turned and run had I been picking up anyone but you."

She laughed, slapped his arm, and then pressed closer to him.

The evening air of summer rushed in through the open, passenger-side window and brought with it the fresh scent of hay and grain as they sped along the freeway between Brigham City and Ogden. They eventually left the farms, orchards, and open country behind.

As they approached the city, Nick said, "I love coming into Salt Lake this time of evening." The mountains to the east formed a beautiful backdrop to the skyline of tall buildings, and the temple was bathed in white light.

Aaron followed the freeway across town to the east bench. "I hope I can find this place," he muttered.

"You've never been there?"

"My roommate told me about it."

"And if we don't ever find it?"

He shrugged. "You don't mind McDonald's, do you?"

Nick looked down at her clothes, glanced over at Aaron, and then pursed her lips. "Are you sure there's even such a place?"

Aaron laughed. "We'll find it. I think."

"You don't sound too confident."

"Right after my mission," he said, chuckling, "I asked this girl out. I'd been home for almost three weeks and still hadn't had a date. I'd been dying to take her out, and I really wanted to impress her.

"There was a place in Provo called Camelot. I had passed it several times, and from the street it looked like a medieval castle with stone walls, turrets, drawbridge, the works. I knew that was the place to impress a girl."

He shook his head. "Here we were all dressed up. I was doing my best to put on airs. I pulled into the parking lot." He laughed. "Camelot turned out to be a fancy apartment complex instead of a restaurant." Nick began to giggle. "I didn't exactly impress anyone. We ended up going to some other place, not nearly as exotic and romantic as I had anticipated Camelot being. That was my last date with her. In fact, that was my last date with anyone for a while. My self-esteem was pretty battered."

"If it will relieve your anxiety any, I don't think the Brass Stag is an apartment complex. Mom told me about it. It sounds like a really neat place."

A few moments later Aaron pointed down the street and announced, "There it is." Both of them spotted the life-size, flood-lit, brass sculpture of a huge bull elk standing on a well-groomed lawn in a grouping of trees. A circular driveway led from the street to the front door of the restaurant, which was covered by a dark green awning.

"We're in luck. There really is a Brass Stag."

An elaborate wrought iron fence surrounding the restaurant contributed to the exclusive feel of the place. As Aaron drove in to the circular drive, Nick gaped at the beautiful grounds. The restaurant was situated in a park-like setting of thick lawns, willow trees, and small ponds.

As they approached the entrance, two young men dressed in dark pants and short, white jackets came out from their station outside the front door.

"Valet parking," Nick commented, glancing over at Aaron. "You're impressing me."

Aaron swallowed hard. "Actually, I'm scaring myself," he muttered. "My roommate didn't say anything about valet parking. Look at those cars," he said, surveying the parking area. "These two guys probably don't know what a Ford or a Chevy is."

Nick pressed her hand to her mouth to stifle a giggle.

"This really isn't funny," Aaron said, trying to sound stern. He shook his head. "I was hoping I could park in an inconspicuous spot and slip into the restaurant without being noticed. Don't get me wrong. I love this old truck, but I'm not sure everyone is able to appreciate its finer qualities. Let's park on the street and walk in."

"Oh, Bear River girls are more sophisticated than that."

Aaron twisted around in his seat just as a black Porsche pulled in behind them. "Well, we're blocked in. I guess we bluff it from here."

Nick put the truck into gear and the Chevy inched forward. "Just keep a straight face, Miss Sophisticated Bear River City woman. Stick your chin out a bit, jab your nose in the air, and unless someone is wearing the crown jewels, don't give them the time of day."

Aaron pulled the Chevy up under the awning covering the restaurant's entrance and stopped. Both valets eyed the truck with obvious disdain. Finally one of them sauntered haughtily to Aaron's side of the truck. "If this is a delivery," he began impatiently, "they are made around—" Then he noticed how Nick and Aaron were dressed. He coughed. "Welcome to the Brass Stag. May I park your . . . " He cleared his throat. "Your vehicle, sir?"

For a moment Aaron looked the valet up and down. "I will appreciate it," he began airily, "if you will park this vehicle very carefully."

"Huh?" The valet pointed at the truck. "This?"

Aaron did his best to look down his nose. He breathed deeply and rolled his eyes. "This is not a common truck."

"What?"

"Do you have any appreciation for vintage vehicles?"

The valet studied the truck and shrugged. "Looks like an old Chevy to me."

Aaron heaved a sigh and turned to Nick. "This *is* the place your father told us about, isn't it?" Without waiting for her response, Aaron turned back to the valet. "I'll park it myself. I can't risk having it damaged."

Just then the other valet stepped to the truck. "What's the matter?"

"Surely *you* know something about antiques." The valet looked questioningly at his companion and then back at Aaron without speaking. Aaron sighed petulantly. "You aren't familiar with this particular model of the 1957 Chevrolet?"

"Well . . . I believe . . . Why, yes, I am." He looked the truck over, searching for some characteristic that would distinguish it as a special model.

"We are in the process of restoring it, and I don't want it banged up." He turned to Nick. "We really should have

brought the Lincoln as your father suggested." Aaron
dropped the keys into the second valet's hand, reached into
his pocket, pulled out a roll of money, peeled off a ten dollar
bill, and pressed it into the young man's hand. "You will
take special care of it, won't you?"

The valet stared down at the ten dollar bill and nodded
his head. "Of course—Sir."

Walking next to Aaron to the entrance of the restaurant, Nick fought to keep from laughing and whispered,
"Ten dollars? I would have parked it for five."

"I would have preferred to have parked it myself for
nothing. But then how does one impress the servants?"

"You're crazy."

"That was the easy part. Now we've got to bluff our way
into the inner sanctuary."

A man in a black suit opened the front door for them,
and they were immediately met by another gentleman,
wearing a tuxedo. "Under what name is the reservation,
sir?" he asked.

"Mr. Aaron James Solinski," Aaron answered, hardly
giving the man a glance. "I hope Father's secretary didn't
forget to make the reservations, too," he muttered.

The man studied a book on the front desk. "I'm sorry,
there doesn't seem to be a reservation for . . . "

"Perhaps it's under Ms. Nadine Jerard," Aaron offered in
an exasperated tone of voice. "It wouldn't surprise me if
Mildred put the reservation under your name. It's like her
to do something like that."

"There is no Ms. Jerard, Sir."

"Oh, I don't believe this," Aaron complained irritably,
turning to Nick. "If Father doesn't fire that woman after
tonight, something is wrong. How can he run a major
corporation with dithering fools like Mildred Weston

disorganizing everything she touches? Nadine, perhaps we should go someplace where. . ."

"I'm sure we can find you a place," the gentleman spoke quickly. "I'll find a table for you immediately."

"I have never worked so hard to keep a straight face," Nick giggled. They were seated at a table next to a bank of picture windows looking out over the city below. The sun had set, but the sky and clouds over the Great Salt Lake were still aglow with fiery reds and deep purples. "I was surprised you didn't lose it," she marveled.

"Dignity," Aaron cautioned haughtily. "Maintain your dignity, Ms. Jerard."

"I didn't know you were such a snob. You play the part all too well. Am I to assume that I'm seeing the real Aaron Solinski?"

He stared at her across the table and then his face broke into a wide grin. "Who knows? But if we can just make it through the meal without slurping our soup or eating our steak with our fingers, we might be able to pull this charade off."

The two looked about the dining area. The tables were draped with white linen cloths and elegantly set with china and silverware. The chairs were all high-backed, and there were real flowers on every table. A number of small lamps gave the darkened room an intimate feel.

"It *is* nice," Nick commented. "A notch or two above Peach City Drive-in. I'm glad I didn't wear my boots." Glancing at the other diners, she asked, "Do we fit in?"

"Sure. The way you look, we're going to have waiters falling all over themselves trying to impress us."

Nick smiled at the compliment. Then, after a moment, she asked, "Is your middle name really *James?*"

"Of course. Sounds sophisticated, doesn't it?"

"Aaron James." She said the name slowly as though savoring it. "I could call you AJ."

Aaron's smile drooped and he shook his head. "No, don't call me AJ. Anything but AJ."

"Why not?"

He hesitated a moment, pondering. "People called my father AJ. There was a time when I wanted to have that name as well." He shook his head. "Not any more."

"You really dislike your father, don't you?" She seemed surprised.

"I try not to like or dislike him. I try not to even think about him."

"But you do think of him."

"Sometimes."

For a long moment Aaron was quiet, rearranging the silverware before him. "When I was growing up, we were quite well-to-do. Dad had a really good job at Motorola. He had a couple of small businesses on the side. I didn't think there was a greater guy in the whole world."

He paused, staring down at the tabletop. Finally he looked up and met Nick's gaze. "Then he walked out on us. He just walked away without looking back."

"Why?"

"There was a woman he knew at work, about ten years younger than he was. Mom tried to keep the marriage together. Nothing helped. He left us. He left the Church. He left everything.

"I remember hoping he would come back. I used to dream he would walk back into our lives." Aaron smiled sardonically, shaking his head. "He never did. Mom ended up marrying Jack Solinski, an old friend of AJ's. Jack was the one who pulled us all through. He and Mom are happily married."

"How long has it been since you've seen him?"

"Thirteen, fourteen, maybe fifteen years. I haven't kept track."

"Do you know where he is or what he's doing?"

He shook his head. "I know he's not married to that woman any more. In fact, he got married a couple of times after that. He left Motorola. Then he ran into some legal problems and lost most everything he had. He even spent a year or so in a medium security prison. I don't know where he is now. Or what he's doing."

"Aren't you curious?"

"I don't want to be curious. He walked out of my life. I don't want him to ever walk back in." He took a deep breath. "But we didn't come here to talk about all of that." He smiled. "What would you like to eat?"

The meal was delicious and quietly relaxing. When they were finished eating, Aaron spoke. "I've been told there's dancing on the next floor. Did you bring your dancing shoes?"

"I'm not much of a dancer," Nick confessed shyly. She smiled. "Maybe that's the reason I always played sports."

"We'll change that. Come on." He reached across the table and took her hand, helping her up.

"I don't know, Aaron. With the exception of some wild experiences in junior high, the only real dancing I've done was in a social dance class I took my first quarter at USU. I pulled a B, but I had to really work at it."

Aaron squeezed her hand and pulled her next to him. "If I can learn with two left feet, you'll be able to remember something from a quarter at USU."

A live band was playing and they started off with a waltz. "You were being too modest," Aaron commented as they glided about the floor.

Her cheeks reddened. "It helps to have a partner who knows what he's doing."

Aaron held her close. Her hair brushed against his cheek, and he realized that this was the first time that they had ever really been close. After several dances they found a small table against the far wall and ordered drinks. "How does this compare to a good hard game of softball or an early morning 10K?" Aaron asked, still holding her hand.

Nick thought for a moment and then smiled across the table at him. "I get a better workout in softball." She squeezed his hand. "But this is more fun. I could do this longer."

Aaron raised his brow and cocked his head to one side. "All right, we'll have to do this again another day."

"I'd love to."

It was after eleven when Nick and Aaron left the Brass Stag and climbed into Aaron's truck. Nick leaned against him and looped her arm through his. "You in the mood for ice cream?" he asked.

"Ice cream? After all that?"

He shrugged. "Dinner's never finished until I've had dessert. There's a fun little place called the Cow's Moo over by the university. It's got the best chocolate sundae in the whole valley. They don't have valet parking, but they have good ice cream."

Nick laughed, a musical kind of laugh. "Then let's go to the Cow's Moo. After the Brass Stag and the Cow's Moo, I'll feel like I've been to the zoo."

Aaron found a parking spot a half block from the ice cream store. He stepped around to Nick's door and opened it. Holding her hand as she stepped down, he felt his heart pound in his chest. As she stepped onto the sidewalk, her heel caught in a crack in the sidewalk and she fell against him. He caught her, took both her arms, and then pulled her close and kissed her once on the lips.

It was hard to tell who was more surprised. For a moment he stood there, his eyes wide and apologetic. She took a quick, involuntary step backward and looked up at him.

"I'm sorry," he mumbled, wetting his lips and stuffing his

hands into his pockets. "That just happened. I wasn't even thinking about it."

"You weren't?"

He shook his head and swallowed hard. "But it did seem like the thing to do."

The two gazed at each other a moment and then Aaron took her hand and started down the street for the Cow's Moo. Inside they sat in a booth, ordered, and began to eat their sundaes in silence.

"I'm sorry about that out there."

Nick looked up. "You are?" Her eyes teased.

"Well, sort of. I mean, I usually don't go around doing that kind of thing. It just seemed the natural thing to do."

"You did take me by surprise."

"Are you upset?"

She thought for a moment. Slowly she shook her head and stirred her dish of ice cream. The color rushed to her cheeks. "Actually," she confessed shyly, "that's the first time I've been kissed."

Aaron looked up. "You've never been kissed before?"

"Not by a guy. I mean, not by anyone who wasn't family."

"No wonder you were shocked. How have you managed that?"

She smiled and shrugged.

"Nobody tried?"

"Oh, one guy tried once, but he was so clumsy about it that he just irritated me. Another guy asked me if he could, and asking me seemed so corny and unromantic that I just flat told him no."

"I'm glad I didn't ask."

"I'm glad you didn't, either."

"And Richard, he didn't ever try?"

"You're getting personal now," she scolded playfully.

Later, as they strolled down the street, Nick held onto Aaron's arm and leaned her head against his shoulder. When they reached the truck, they stopped and faced each other. Aaron took both her hands and leaned forward and kissed her once on the lips, this time more slowly.

"Was that an accident, too?" Nick asked him, smiling.

He shook his head. "No, I thought about that one. I've been thinking of that one ever since the first one." He kissed her again.

It took her a moment to catch her breath and then she whispered, "I can remember one softball game that was better."

"Well, I can keep trying until I get it right," Aaron came back softly, smiling and holding her close. "Actually, I like the practice."

They were quiet as they drove out of Salt Lake and headed for home. When they finally pulled into the yard at Nick's house, it was nearly two o'clock. Aaron looked at his watch, then took Nick's hand and asked, "What are you doing tomorrow night, Nadine?"

"Well—"

"Tell him you can't."

"But I told him—"

"Tell him you don't want to."

"I guess I *don't* want to. Not after tonight."

"Tell him."

"Are things moving too fast for us?" she asked.

"They've always been moving fast. We just didn't know it. Tomorrow night?"

"Where?"

Aaron shrugged. "Any place with you."

"If we're not careful, we'll get the boys worrying about us."

"Tomorrow night?" He glanced at his watch. "I guess I mean tonight."

She smiled and nodded. "Tonight then."

Chapter Fourteen

Nick was doing some filing in the office when the phone rang. "J. T. Overson Construction," she answered formally. "May I help you?"

"Are you about ready to wrap things up?"

"Aaron," she exclaimed, glancing over at Theresa Porter, who worked with her. Theresa smiled, and Nick winked.

"I'll give you a ride home. Give me fifteen minutes."

Hanging up the phone, Nick leaned back in her chair, closed her eyes, took a deep breath, and sighed softly.

"You've got fifteen minutes till quitting time," Theresa reminded her, nodding toward the clock.

"I don't know if I can make it fifteen minutes. I have so many butterflies, I can't swallow."

"You've got it bad."

"And it feels so good. Theresa," she asked, becoming serious, "do you think twenty-six is too old?"

"That depends on how mature *you* are."

"Oh, I'm very mature," she answered staidly. "On a maturity scale I'm between thirty and thirty-five." She laughed.

"Sounds to me like you should find some old widower, someone a little closer to your maturity age. Aaron will think you're his mother. Isn't Jeremiah about twenty-six?"

"Oh, but Aaron isn't Jeremiah. Take my word for it."

Shaking her head, Theresa remarked, "I just hope you're not running faster than you've got strength."

"I'm in great shape. I haven't even started to sprint yet."

A few minutes later an air horn blared from the street and a giant J. T. Overson Construction dump truck pulled up to the curb in front of the office. Aaron jumped down from the cab of the truck and came into the office carrying a long white box. Stepping to Nick's desk, he pulled his hard hat from his head and bowed deeply. "Special delivery for Ms. Nadine 'Nick' Jerard."

Giggling, Nick said, "I thought you were going to give me a ride home."

Aaron nodded toward the street, where he had left the truck running. "When was the last time you had the pleasure of riding in a J. T. Overson dump truck?"

"Never."

"Today's your lucky day."

"J. T. let you borrow his truck to take me home? As long as he was in a generous mood, why didn't you ask for his Cadillac?"

"Actually, there's this guy out past your place who wants a load of pea gravel. I figured as long as I was making the trip, I'd stop by and give you a lift. That way you wouldn't have to hitchhike."

"You're crazy, Aaron Solinski." He shrugged and set the white oblong box on her desk.

"What's this?" she asked.

"Open it."

Nick loosened the huge pink bow. Her hands shook slightly as she pulled the lid off and pushed back the green floral paper inside, revealing a dozen, long-stemmed, pink roses. She gasped and looked up at Aaron, who was fidgeting with his hat in his hands. She reached in and touched one of the roses.

"According to a great philosopher, some things can only be said with roses. I had a lot to say. And it had to be said in pink."

"Pink?"

"I think Nadine Jerard needs a little more pink in her life."

"They're beautiful," she whispered, picking them up and breathing in their rich fragrance.

"Well, we better get going," Aaron burst out suddenly, putting his hat on his head.

Nick looked up at him. "You're serious about taking me home in that?" He nodded.

"I didn't bring my hiking boots. I don't know if I can climb that high," she said, studying the truck's huge cab.

"I'll help you."

"I want you to know that I'd never do this with anyone else."

"Good." He turned to Theresa. "You want to come, too."

She shook her head. "I think I'll have just as much fun watching the two of you drive away in J. T.'s truck."

A few minutes later Nick and Aaron were driving down the main street in Tremonton. As he worked through the gears, Aaron said, "Maybe we should have taken this to the Brass Stag."

"There's always a next time. You'll have to speak to J. T. and reserve it."

"I'll drop you off at your place and then be back later."

"Later?" she asked. "For what?"

Aaron stared over at her. "Just because I give you a ride home in an expensive machine doesn't mean I'm going to let you out of your training. You've got USU's track team to think about."

"You don't let anything interfere with your coaching, do you?"

"We're making a champion out of you."

Standing in the long shadows of the poplar trees, with deep, gold bars of sunlight all about them, Nick and Aaron rested on the bridge after her workout and tossed pebbles into the water below. Nick leaned back against a steel beam, took in a huge breath of air, and closed her eyes. "I feel so good," she said contentedly.

"You can say that after running five miles and doing ten minutes of windsprints?" Without opening her eyes she nodded her head. Aaron studied her a moment. Then he leaned over and kissed her.

Nick swallowed and caught her breath. "Is this part of our workout, Coach?"

He smiled. "If it isn't, it should be." He kissed her again, this time longer.

"Will it improve my conditioning?" she asked.

He thought a moment. "This kind of therapy is still being evaluated, but anything that feels this good has to be beneficial."

"You're the coach. I'll take your word for it."

They both laughed and started for home, hand in hand. "What are you doing Friday?" Aaron asked.

"You haven't told me yet."

"We need to break down this 'dumb athlete' stereotype. How would you like to go hear the Utah Symphony?"

"I can't picture you showing up at a symphony concert," she teased.

"Have you ever been?" he asked.

She became serious, put her chin out and her nose up and answered, "Well, of course. You should have grown up in Bear River City. You would have received plenty of culture." She laughed. "Hey, guess what? J. T. is sending me on a road job."

"A road job?"

"I've been telling him that there isn't anything his men are doing that I can't do better."

Aaron smiled. "You said that to J. T.?"

Nick nodded. "He tried to humor me by saying he couldn't afford to lose good office help. He even upped my wages. He should have. This is the third summer I've worked for him. But I kept badgering him. This morning he said he is going to send me out for three or four weeks to work as a flagman, just so I'll stop pestering him. He thinks one day in the sun, and I'll be ready to return to the comforts of an air-conditioned office."

"This road job wouldn't be up around Preston, Idaho, would it?"

"How'd you know?"

Aaron grinned. "My foreman told me this afternoon that he's sending me up there next week. It has to be the same job. He said the company is going to put us up in motels since it's an eighty-mile drive from here to there."

Nick shook her head. "I have an aunt who lives in Preston. I'll stay with her during the week and come back on weekends."

"Maybe we'd better check it out before we go charging up there," Aaron said. "Let's drive up on Sunday."

It was growing dark when Aaron finally entered his sister's house to shower and eat supper. Regina was finishing the dishes when he came in. "You're late," she commented. He picked up a carrot stick from the table and began munching it. "With Nick?" He smiled and nodded. "You're serious, Aaron."

He stuffed the rest of the carrot stick in his mouth and chewed. "Maybe."

"Do you ever think of Brittany any more?"

He considered the question a moment. "For a long time I didn't know if I would ever get over Brittany. But I didn't feel what I feel with Nick. We're different, but something clicks with us."

"I saw this coming the first evening you asked me about her."

Aaron chuckled. "Maybe I did, too. Oh, by the way, I'll be gone next week. We're doing a stretch of road up in Idaho."

"Where?" she asked, wiping the tabletop with a wet cloth.

"Just outside of Preston."

Surprised, Regina straightened up, the dish cloth dangling in her hand. "You ever been there?" Aaron asked.

"Sure. A few times."

"What's it like?"

For a moment she didn't answer. "It's a pretty place, a lot of nice little farms around."

"Nick and I are going to drive up on Sunday and go to church there."

"You'll like it."

"Nick's going to be working there too."

"Nick?"

"She badgered J. T. into giving her a real job, out working on the road." He laughed.

For a few moments they were both quiet. Regina finally broke the silence. "Aaron, do you ever wonder about Daddy?"

"AJ?" Regina hesitated and then nodded. "I try not to," he muttered tiredly. He paused a moment and then asked, "Why do you bring up AJ?"

"I've been thinking about him lately." She paused. "Would you ever like to see him?"

Aaron studied his sister without answering.

"I think he'd like to see you. Maybe now's a good time. After all—"

"Regina," he responded, making an attempt at patience, "I've spent a long time chasing off the old ghosts of AJ Tippets. I don't want to invite them back."

"You're the only one in the family who hasn't had contact with Daddy. Even Mom has."

"That's fine with me."

"I was just wondering," Regina remarked quietly.

Aaron shrugged and shook his head. "If I did go out of my way to see him, it would be just to satisfy a morbid curiosity. Maybe if I could see him without having to talk to him or without him seeing me it wouldn't be so bad." He quickly shook his head again. "But I think I'm content to leave AJ alone. He's done that long enough for me. I'm happy to return the favor."

The morning, though mildly warm, was pleasant as Nick and Aaron drove the Civic north out of Logan and toward Preston. With the windows down, the fresh air blew in over them, bringing with it the rich summer aroma of newly cut hay. The countryside between Logan and Preston was a patchwork of fields of alfalfa, meadow grass, yellow bearded barley, tall tassled corn, and golden wheat. There was a scattering of farm homes, sheds, and barns along the way. It was Sunday and most of the tractors and farm equipment lay idle in the fields.

"I've always loved this drive," Nick commented, smiling and reaching out the window so the rush of air could brush over her bare arm. "Every time we'd come up to see Aunt

Marge, I'd think I'd like to move up this way. I did tell you that she invited us to dinner, didn't I?"

Aaron nodded and smiled, enjoying Nick's girlish enthusiasm. "I hope your adventure as a flagwoman doesn't taint all these happy memories you have of Preston."

Nick shook her head and tousled her hair. "Not a chance. Aunt Marge has been alone since Uncle Ross passed away ten years ago. Even if I hate the job, I'll love being with her. I told her that we'd meet her at the church."

"Can you find this church, or is there only one in all of Preston?"

"For your information, Preston is a very impressive community. Actually, it's rather big. For a small town. Lots bigger than Bear River."

"Not bigger than Bear River?" Aaron gasped mockingly.

"All right, Mr. Smart Mouth. Leave your cynicism home this trip. There are several churches in Preston, but this one is right on State Street."

"State Street?" Aaron looked over at Nick. "That definitely sounds impressive."

"You have a very bad attitude, Mr. Solinski." She faked a frown. "I am not impressed by uppity people. And this morning you are horribly uppity."

"My apology." He smiled. "I'll get rid of my airs. And my bad attitude."

Preston was quiet and peaceful on Sunday morning. State Highway 191 changed to State Street as it passed through town. With the exception of a half dozen parked cars, State Street was practically deserted, lined with high-front stores pressed together, their windows filled with quaint displays and banners. There were wooden planters along the sidewalk, each one containing a small tree and colorful petunias. Nick and Aaron read the store signs as they drove slowly along: O. P. Skaggs, Kings, The Ginger-bread Shoppe, Main Street Grill.

"At the risk of making something resembling an apology, I must admit that I am impressed," Aaron said quietly, gazing out the window and enjoying the enchantment that was Preston on a lazy Sunday morning. He reached over and took Nick's hand. "Thanks for coming."

She smiled and wagged a finger at him. "I hope you're sincere."

"Sincere is what I do best."

The church, a red brick structure with decorative square white pillars in front, was on the north end of town. "There's Aunt Marge on the front steps!" Nick called out excitedly.

"So, Nadine, this is your young friend," Marge Eaton said and smiled approvingly as she held out her hand to Aaron. She was in her middle sixties. She looked at Aaron closely, and he took note of her soft, blue eyes. She had a disarming smile and kind, gentle features. "I knew you had to be rather special or you wouldn't have caught Nadine's eye in the first place."

"Aunt Marge!"

"Oh, she's a fussy young lady, if you haven't already noticed."

"Aunt Marge," Nick scolded, "I didn't drive all this way to be embarrassed."

Still holding Aaron's hand, Marge patted his cheek. "I'm glad you came. And don't pay a lot of attention to a doting, old woman. I just want to make certain that my favorite niece doesn't run off with—"

"Aunt Marge! Really!"

As Nick and Aaron were leaving the chapel after the block of meetings, the bishop shook Aaron's hand. As he did so, his mouth dropped open and shock registered plainly on his face.

"Bishop Tucker," Aunt Marge spoke up, "this is Aaron Solinski, a friend of my niece, Nadine Jerard."

"Oh," the bishop responded slowly, releasing his grip on Aaron's hand. "You're the spitting image of an old missionary companion of mine—an Elder Tippets I served with in Mexico City. In fact, he lives in Preston now, but I thought . . . " Bishop Tucker caught himself and smiled. "I'm pleased to meet you, Aaron. Solinski, is it?" Aaron nodded. "I hope you'll visit us again."

Aaron was solemn and quiet as they drove away from the church toward Marge's home, a split-level house with white siding surrounded by a well-manicured lawn and carefully trimmed shrubs.

"Aaron?" Nick asked gently, reaching over and touching the back of his hand.

Aaron sat rigidly with his jaw clamped shut. Gripping the steering wheel, he looked away.

"Do you think this Tippets . . . is your father?"

Aaron heaved a sigh. "AJ grew up down in Hyrum, the other side of Logan. It might be him. It probably is. He served a mission in Mexico, and he's about the same age as Bishop Tucker." Aaron rubbed his chin with his thumb. "I think Regina tried to tell me the other night."

"Do you want to see him?"

"No!" The response was quick, sharp, and definite.

Aaron spoke little through dinner. Later, as the three cleared the table, he asked, "Mrs. Eaton, do you know AJ Tippets?" He didn't look at her as he spoke. He was gathering the silverware from the table and kept his gaze downward.

"Yes, I know AJ," Marge answered quietly. She hesitated a moment and then continued. "He came to Preston two or three years ago. Maybe longer. He lives alone in a small house a couple of blocks from here. He's fixed my stove and washer and done some work on my roof. He's always willing to lend a hand. Never charges much. I've heard that he's quite educated."

"He has a master's degree in engineering," Aaron commented.

"You know him?"

"At one time he was my father. A long time ago."

She studied Aaron. "It's been a while since you've seen him?"

Aaron nodded.

"Bishop Tucker and he were old missionary companions. AJ was an . . . an alcoholic when he first came to Preston."

"He was a drunk?" Aaron's surprise was obvious.

"He came hoping Bishop Tucker could help him. Bishop Tucker has done wonderful things with him."

As Nick and Aaron drove out of Preston that afternoon, Nick asked, "Don't you want to at least drive by your dad's place?"

"Nick, AJ is like a black hole inside me, sucking away at all the good things I want in life."

"AJ Tippets can't take anything from you, Aaron."

"At one time I hated him," Aaron said. "While I was on my mission in Peru, I realized that I couldn't hate on one side and preach the gospel of love on the other. I have worked hard not to hate him. I just don't want to see him."

Aaron smiled sadly. "When Jack married Mom, I was a rotten, hate-filled kid. The last thing I wanted was another dad. Any other guy would have written me off as a lost cause, but Jack stayed with me, always patient, always kind, always loving.

"I stole a four-wheeler when I was thirteen. Some cop saw me and chased me. I rolled the four-wheeler and busted myself up pretty good. I remember waking up in the hospital with Jack sitting by the bed holding my hand. Crying. And praying." Aaron swallowed. "He told the Lord how much he loved me, that he would try harder to be a better dad, if only he could have another chance."

Aaron was quiet a moment. "AJ didn't sit by my bedside and pray for another chance. Instead, he sent me a get-well card and signed his name," Aaron said bitterly. "Six months later Jack adopted me with AJ's consent."

"You're lucky," Nick commented.

"Lucky?"

"I grew up without a dad too. Some of us don't have a Jack Solinski who steps in." She paused, then added, "If I had a chance to see my father, I would."

"Your dad was killed. He didn't just walk away from you."

"But I still had to grow up without him. The disadvantages were there for me too. I had to go on. Just like you have to. If we're not careful, we can blame a person or a thing for everything that's gone wrong in our lives."

"You think that's what I've done with AJ?"

"Maybe."

"Nick, I think I've reconciled myself to the loss. I just *don't* want to reintroduce AJ Tippets into my life."

Regina was in the living room when Aaron slipped into the house. "How did it go?" she questioned.

"Interesting." He dropped into the overstuffed chair. "You know AJ lives in Preston, don't you?"

"I tried to tell you," she explained quietly.

"I ran into one of his old missionary companions, Bishop Tucker." He hesitated. "Have you seen AJ recently?"

Regina nodded. "A couple of months ago. He stopped by for a few minutes." She studied her brother. "Aaron, you ought to see him. Don't do to him what he did to you."

Chapter Fifteen

"Had any doubts about being a liberated woman on a construction crew?" Aaron joked as he tossed his hard hat aside and dropped down in the shade of a pine tree next to Nick, who had already torn into her lunch.

"A mistake here and there, but everybody survived."

"The guy in the Ford Bronco almost didn't," Aaron commented, grinning and biting into his ham sandwich. "I thought Harrison was going to have to pry that Bronco out of his grill."

"I was hoping no one had noticed," Nick muttered sheepishly.

Aaron laughed. "That Bronco driver noticed." He shook his head. "He must have been a little shaken by the whole experience because he stopped down the road and let his wife drive."

"Is that all you noticed today?"

Aaron smiled and nudged Nick with his elbow. "Actually, I noticed that you were the best-looking flag lady I've ever seen on a construction crew."

"Your flattery is wasted. Especially after your criticism."

The two ate silently, taking in the beauty of the low rolling hills covered with brush, pine, and aspen trees. "What do you have going tonight?" Aaron questioned as he wadded up his sack.

"A long bath."

"And after that?"

"Oh, one of the guys on the crew is taking me some-place," she answered casually.

"Who?" The question was quick, touched with surprised hurt.

Nick was serious for a moment and then her wide grin crinkled her sun-blushed face. "Well, I was kind of hoping *you* were going to take me someplace. After all, I am all alone in this town without a friend to turn to." She grabbed his arm, squeezed, pressed her cheek against his shoulder and laughed. Aaron smiled. "Seven-thirty. And don't eat dinner."

Dressed casually in a pair of blue jeans and a T-shirt, Nick was waiting on Marge's front steps when Aaron pulled up. "You must be hungry. You're out here waiting for me."

"Famished."

"What's your pleasure?" Aaron asked as they headed for downtown Preston.

"What are my choices?"

"Anything Preston has to offer."

"Maybe we'd better take a quick tour and see what there is."

A few minutes later Aaron turned to Nick. "Unless I missed something, we have Arctic Circle, Pizza Villa, the Main Street Grill, Juniper Upstairs, or Big J's Drive-in. What sounds good?"

Nick grinned. "Surprise me."

"I've got a craving for pizza."

"Pizza sounds great."

It was eight-thirty when they left the Pizza Villa. The sun had almost disappeared, and a refreshing evening breeze stirred the air. Nick and Aaron strolled west through the city park, where two softball games were in progress. The tennis court was occupied by two older couples. A group was finishing a picnic under the trees. The county fairgrounds and rodeo arena west of the park were deserted.

Later they walked arm in arm up and down State Street, peering in the windows of the locked shops and stores, eventually stopping on the imposing steps of the huge Franklin County Courthouse. Bright lights bathed the entire front of the building, making it an impressive sight.

"I could live here," Aaron said with satisfaction.

"I don't think they allow lawyers to become citizens of nice communities like Preston. You know how they—" Her sentence exploded into a squeal as Aaron grabbed her about the waist and began to tickle her. "Aaron, I'll scream," she warned, attempting to wriggle free. "And everybody in town will come charging down here to see what you're doing to a helpless girl."

After a few moments of playful struggle, the two relaxed and stood with their arms looped comfortably around the other's waist and smiling at each other. "Maybe I won't be a lawyer when I come here," Aaron commented huskily.

"What would you be?"

Taking a deep breath and looking about him, he shrugged and answered. "Maybe I'll just be a dump truck driver. Or maybe I'll open a nice little hot dog stand right over there across the street."

"A hot dog stand? That's interesting. Will you need a partner?"

Aaron smiled. "Of course, I could do something more practical and go over to the high school and become an English teacher." He looked down at her. "By the way, do you have something against lawyers?"

"Depends on who the lawyer is."

For a moment they smiled at each other, and then slowly their eyes closed and they came together in a gentle kiss. "I wonder if we should do this in a more private place,"

Nick said softly as they separated. "I'm not sure I feel comfortable here on the front steps of the courthouse with the floodlights glaring so brightly." She reached up and kissed him again.

"Actually, I think we're alone. I'll bet the rest of the citizens have all retired for the night," Aaron said.

Aunt Marge's porch light was still on when Aaron walked Nick to the front door. "You know," Nick remarked quietly, leaning her head against Aaron's shoulder as they walked, "this afternoon, as the sun burned down a little hotter, and the dust got a little thicker, and I didn't think I'd ever feel clean again, I began thinking how nice it had been in J. T. Overson's office, answering the telephone in air-conditioned comfort. But after tonight, I think I'm going to like this . . . " She paused and took a deep breath. "This road building business."

"I think your brothers might caution you not to fraternize with the crew. You know how construction guys are."

"The fraternizing is what I like best."

Talk turned to AJ Tippets just once that first week. "Don't you think we ought to stop by your dad's place?" Nick asked on Tuesday evening as Aaron was preparing to leave for the night. "I mean, you're right here just a block or so away. Stop by and see him. I'd like to meet him."

Aaron turned away, took a deep breath and then let it out slowly. He rubbed the palms of his hands together in front of him and gazed up at the night sky. "I don't think I can, Nick."

"Aaron, he's your dad. I'll bet he'd love to see you."

"I'll have to admit that I've thought about it. I guess I'm curious." He turned back to her. "But after this many years of trying to block him out, I don't know if I can bring myself to just walk up to him. Maybe sometime. But not right now."

"I'll go with you if it makes it easier."

Aaron took her hand. "Thanks," he said. "I'll think about it. But I'm not ready yet."

Nick and Aaron were together every night that first week. Once they drove up through the mountains northeast of town for an evening picnic. One night they ate at Juniper Upstairs. Aunt Marge invited Aaron over twice for dinner. When they weren't exploring Preston or the surrounding country, they visited in Aunt Marge's backyard.

"How did you like Preston?" Regina asked Aaron on Friday evening after he returned to Tremonton for the weekend.

Aaron smiled and poured himself a glass of grape juice. "I don't remember much about Preston. But there's this girl on the crew . . . " He shook his head, drank his juice, and grinned over at his sister.

"I'm beginning to wonder if my little brother is going to be able to leave this young country girl behind. You go back to Arizona in a few weeks."

"I'll worry about that in a few weeks. Besides . . . "

"Besides what?"

"Oh, nothing. I was just thinking. You don't always have to leave people behind."

Wednesday of the following week the foreman of the crew closed the job down thirty minutes early because a thunderstorm was blowing in. Nick climbed into the Civic next to Aaron. "Looks like we're in for a gully washer," Aaron commented, glancing at a darkening sky that was crackling with lightning.

Five miles from Preston the downpour came in a torrent

while thunder and lightning crashed and flashed about them. Then suddenly the car swerved and careened off the road and plowed harmlessly into a thick patch of tall weeds.

"Are you okay?" Aaron asked, turning to Nick, whose face had turned white.

Nick remained frozen for a moment with her eyes wide and mouth open. Then she relaxed and exhaled loudly. "What happened?"

"I'll take a look." Aaron was back in a few moments, rain mixed with dirt dripping off his hard hat and running down his face. He was completely soaked. "The back tire blew. And that's not the worst of it. The spare's flat. I was planning on fixing it this week."

"Good timing," Nick said, smiling and looking about as the rain pounded down on the car. "What do we do?"

"Wait the storm out and then hope someone stops and picks us up."

Five minutes later an old, white, Dodge pickup truck pulled in alongside them. The driver rolled his window down and shouted above the pounding rain, "Need some help?"

"We've got a flat. And a bad spare. Which way you headed?"

"I'll go wherever you need to go for help."

"Can you give us a lift into Preston?"

"Jump in. Throw the spare in the back."

Nick climbed into the cab of the Dodge while Aaron wrestled the spare out of his trunk and threw it into the back of the pickup. Then, dripping water, he slid in next to Nick.

The driver was an older man. He was wearing dirty clothes. His thin, calloused hands were covered with grease and grime, and a well-used John Deere cap was pulled down over his graying hair, shading his bristled brows and gray eyes.

"You came along just in time," Aaron commented thankfully. "I wasn't looking forward to trudging through this rain all the way into Preston."

The man chuckled but kept his eyes on the wet road ahead as the wiper blades swished frantically to clear the pounding rain from the windshield. "Where you coming from?"

"We're working on a road construction job back a ways."

They exchanged small talk for a few minutes and then the older man remarked, "I've got a little shop over behind my place. I could probably help you fix that spare."

"Oh, I wouldn't want to bother you. Nick and I can—"

"No bother. Don't have anything else to do this afternoon. Not with this rain coming down the way it is. I was helping a fellow put in a septic tank, but the rain put a stop to that. We'll fix the spare and then take it back to your car."

The Dodge pulled up in front of a run-down frame house, miniature in size. Its pink paint was old and cracking. The white paint on the window frames was chipped and flaking off. The pitched roof was covered with asphalt shingles that were beginning to curl at the edges. Faded, metal awnings shaded the front windows, and a small log planter ran the entire width of the house, but its dirt was barren. There was a corner porch leading to the front door. The concrete porch steps were cracked and crumbling. In front were three giant poplar trees, and behind the house was an unpainted work shed almost as big as the house itself.

Fifteen minutes later the spare was repaired and inflated, and the three drove back in the truck to the disabled Civic. The rain had diminished to a mere sprinkle, and the sun was beginning to peek through the departing clouds above the western hills.

"Well, we sure appreciate you helping us out," Aaron

offered gratefully as he straightened up after putting the spare on. "I'd like to pay you." He reached for his wallet.

The man held up his hands and shook his head. "You needed help. I was glad I came along." He pinched his nose with his thumb and forefinger and shook his head. "I'm an old fix-it man," he said, smiling. "If something's broken, I try to find a way to fix it. If someone needs a hand, I try to lend it. I don't do this kind of work for money."

"Well, thanks," Nick said. "Maybe we can return the favor." She held out her hand. "We didn't even introduce ourselves. I'm Nadine Jerard. People call me Nick. And this is Aaron Solinski." She turned and nodded to Aaron, who held out his hand.

The old man's smile disappeared and his gray eyes narrowed as he studied Aaron. "I'm AJ Tippets," he said hoarsely.

For a long, torturous moment no one spoke. Aaron slowly withdrew his outstretched hand and pushed it into his back pocket. Aaron and AJ faced each other. Nick, an uncomfortable and uncertain bystander, looked back and forth between the two men without speaking.

AJ raised a trembling hand to his unshaven chin and stroked the gray and black bristles growing there. Then he swallowed and ran his tongue over his dry lips. "Well, Aaron, I . . . didn't recognize you."

"No, I guess you wouldn't," Aaron responded gravely. "It's been a few years."

Embarrassment colored AJ's dark face. His gaze darted to the ground at Aaron's feet. "I didn't know you were up this way. The last I heard you were back in Arizona."

"I've moved around a bit. I'm surprised you even knew I was in Arizona." The bitterness was unmasked. "Actually, I'm a little surprised that you even knew I was around at all."

The two men stared at each other for a long moment. Aaron was the first to move. He reached out and took Nick by the arm. "It's getting late." He turned his back to AJ as he helped Nick into the car. Before closing Nick's door, he spoke one last time to AJ. "Thanks for helping. It's nice to know that there's someone out here who's not afraid to stop and help a complete stranger."

The ride back to Preston was quiet. Aaron stared straight ahead. Nick gazed out the window as the green, rain-drenched countryside whipped past. When they reached Marge Eaton's house, Aaron stepped out, walked around to Nick's door, and helped her out.

"Aaron," Nick said softly, "I'm sorry."

"There's nothing for you to be sorry about."

"I guess I'm sorry that everything had to happen. I don't mean today. I mean everything before."

"Well, it happened. I can't change that. No one can."

"It was nice of him to stop."

"Yeah," Aaron agreed, nodding his head. "It's wonderful that he could stop and help a stranger fix a flat but couldn't bother with his own family. I'm touched by his charitable service. It makes me feel a whole lot better."

"Are you coming over this evening? We could talk."

Aaron thought a moment. "If you don't mind . . . " He bit down on his lower lip. "Nick, I kind of feel like I need to do some thinking. It's not that I . . . "

"I understand," Nick soothed, touching and then squeezing his forearm.

The following evening Aaron drove over to Marge's for dinner. As he pulled up, Nick came out of the house carrying a tray covered with a white cloth.

"What are we going to do, eat out here on the front lawn?" Aaron kidded.

Nick smiled. "I was taking this over to . . . an old friend. I didn't expect you quite so early."

"I'm always early when there's food. Hop in the car. Where do you need to go?"

Nick sat uneasily next to Aaron as she gave him directions. As they turned the corner, she nodded her head and said quietly, "It's the little pink one."

Aaron stopped the car half a block from the house. "I had planned to come alone," Nick explained without looking at Aaron. She cleared her throat. "He did us a favor, Aaron. I'd like to return the favor." She hesitated and then burst out in frustration, "Aaron, I'll admit I don't know everything that happened between you and your dad. The bad things I don't even want to know. But the only experience I've had with AJ Tippets was yesterday. I want to tell him thanks."

Aaron sat in the car, staring down the street toward AJ's house, which was almost hidden by the poplar trees growing along the street. Finally he put the car in gear, drove slowly down the street, and parked in front of the house.

"Do you want to come in?" Nick asked. He shook his head. "Do you mind helping me out?"

Aaron stepped out and opened Nick's door. As he did, the front door to the house opened, and AJ came out and started down the narrow, cracked walk that cut across his patch of neglected, shaggy lawn. Aaron stood uneasily as he watched the old man's approach.

"You didn't have to do this, young lady." He smiled at Nick, then glanced cautiously at Aaron. "When you came over last night with the loaf of bread, I thought that was plenty of thanks. But dinner. I'm not used to such kind treatment."

"Oh, Mr. Tippets, it was no trouble at all. We had plenty of food fixed for dinner this evening. I hope it's still hot."

Nick started up the walk. AJ hesitated and turned back
to Aaron. "Would you like to come in?" It was more a plea
than a question.

"You can help me, Aaron," Nick called over her shoulder. "Catch the door for me."

Reluctantly Aaron started up the walk ahead of AJ and
Nick and held open the door and then followed them into
the house.

Just inside the front door was the living room. A lumpy
couch, an overstuffed chair, a scarred coffee table, an end
table with a lopsided lamp on it, and a small bookcase filled
the living room. A few clothes were scattered about, as well
as magazines and books. The carpet was an old, tromped-
down, green and gold shag that cried for a good shampoo-
ing. Off the living room was a tiny kitchen. A full-sized
fridge in the corner dwarfed everything else there—a small
table draped with a red and white checkered oil cloth, three
mismatched chairs, a narrow kitchen sideboard and cabi-
nets, all painted with the same thick, light blue enamel, and
a doll-size porcelain sink. The sagging floor was covered
with black and white checkered linoleum.

"It's not much," AJ apologized, referring to his modest
home, "but an old single guy like me doesn't need much.
There are a couple of bedrooms down the hall. I've got
plenty of room."

Nick set the tray of food on the kitchen table and pulled
back the white cloth. "Sure smells and looks good," AJ commented. "I don't know how to thank you."

Aaron studied AJ. He looked different today. His clothes
were clean—a pair of tan slacks and a white T-shirt. He was
clean-shaven, and his graying hair, which was a little shaggy
about the ears and on the back of his neck, had been combed
back. His cheeks were sunken and gaunt. Aaron hadn't
noticed it the day before, but he could see a slight resem-

blance between this man and the photograph that he had kept on his dresser as a young boy. He wasn't sure where that photograph had ended up. All he remembered was taking it down a few months before Jack Solinski had adopted him.

"Do you want to sit down for a moment?" AJ invited, pulling out two of the chairs and nervously brushing off bread crumbs with the back of his hand.

"Aunt Marge is waiting for us," Nick smiled. "Thanks again. I'll come back later for the dishes."

As Nick and Aaron started for the door, AJ called out suddenly, "Aaron, I . . . " His words died in midsentence. Aaron stopped and turned. "You're welcome any time." His face wrinkled in a pained grimace. "I don't know what to say after so . . . " The words faded into silence.

"Maybe after this many years, the less said the better," Aaron answered, stepping out the door.

"He's changed. It's no wonder I didn't recognize him," Aaron commented as they pulled away and headed to Marge's house. "I didn't remember him being so thin. He was more muscular back then. Yesterday I figured he was a guy about sixty-five. AJ's only in his fifties. I wonder what's happened to him."

The meal at Marge's was a quiet one. Afterward Nick and Aaron took a walk, eventually ending up in front of the old Jefferson School, a three-story, brick structure with the date 1883 prominently displayed in front.

"A lot has happened over the years," Nick remarked quietly. "You're both different."

Aaron heaved a sigh. "When I saw AJ yesterday and knew who he was, I tried to call back the hate. I used to imagine what I'd tell AJ if I ever came face-to-face with him. I practiced some pretty cruel, cutting remarks." He shook his head. "The man I saw yesterday wasn't the same man who left his family almost twenty years ago. That man was strong and handsome. The man I see now is old and broken-down. Yesterday and today, I didn't have the stomach to say any of those harsh things."

"Talk to him. Regardless of what has happened, he's still your father."

"Nick, maybe there's not anything there that I can hate. Maybe I don't even want to hate him, but I don't want to go back to him, either."

"Maybe going to him will help you as much as AJ."

"I guess I'll never know."

"You've got to know. Maybe he'd like to go back and change things as much as you. Why not just let the past go?"

"How do you do that after seventeen years?"

"You forgive him. You wipe the slate clean."

Aaron laughed bitterly. "That's a lot to ask."

Nick reached out and touched Aaron's hand. "There's a time when every one of us will ask to have the slate wiped clean."

"I haven't piled up the kind of debt that AJ has."

"The size of the debt doesn't make any difference, Aaron. All of us have a debt. Do you want God to make you beg to have your slate wiped clean? Do you want to have to beg like you want AJ to beg you?"

"It's different, Nick."

"Is it, Aaron? Or do you just want an exception?"

Chapter Sixteen

Friday afternoon, just before quitting time, Aaron's dump truck broke down. He stayed late helping to get it in condition for work Monday morning. He had planned to drive Nick back to Bear River that evening, although he never actually made arrangements with her. It was a little after seven when he knocked on Marge's door, still dressed in his dirty work clothes.

"Hello, Aaron," Marge greeted cheerily. "They finally let you off. Nick was wondering if you would have to work all night."

"I was starting to wonder myself. Is Nick here?"

"Oh, an old friend of hers dropped by and offered to drive her home."

"A friend?" Aaron questioned.

"A young man. I was hurrying out the door to make it to the store, so the introduction was rather rushed. I don't remember the name. He seemed to be an old family friend who happened to be up this way and offered to take Nadine home. She wasn't sure how long you would be."

Aaron laughed. "That was probably smart of her. The boss told me to leave the truck and let the mechanic look at it tomorrow, or I'd still be out there. Hey, thanks, Mrs. Eaton. I'll see you next week."

Aaron's drive to Bear River was lonely. He had grown accustomed to Nick's cheery companionship. It was

164

approaching nine o'clock when he rushed into Regina's kitchen, said hi to her and the kids, grabbed something to eat, and then jumped into the shower before hurrying over to Nick's. Joseph answered the door.

"Hi, is Nick still up?"

Joseph hesitated, cast a quick glance behind him and then nodded. "Yeah, she's . . . still up. It's a little late."

Aaron laughed as Joseph opened the door wider and motioned for Aaron to come in. "I got held up. I wasn't sure they were going to let me go home at all."

"We're all in the living room," Joseph said.

Aaron immediately noticed the young man sitting next to Nick on the sofa.

"Hey, Aaron," Jared called out. "Come in and meet Richard." The young man sitting next to Nick pushed himself to his feet and held out his hand in greeting, smiling innocently. "Aaron, this is Richard Robbins. Richard, this is Aaron Solinski, a friend of the family. He and I worked together."

"Nice to meet you," Richard said, pumping Aaron's hand enthusiastically. He was two or three inches taller than Aaron but more slender. He was handsome, much more so than Aaron had expected. His blond hair was clipped short, and his whole person had that fresh-scrubbed, innocent, just-released missionary look.

"Richard just got off his mission in Japan." Jared explained. "His folks picked him up in Salt Lake this morning. He drove up to Preston this afternoon and surprised Nick. She hadn't expected him home for a couple more weeks. Richard's still experiencing culture shock."

"You can say that again." Richard sat back down beside Nick and rested his hand on her knee.

"Hey, sit down, Aaron," Jared offered, grabbing a chair and placing it on the opposite side of the room from Nick. "Richard's been telling us about Japan."

Aaron smiled, shook his head, and started backing toward the door. "No, I've got to get going. It's late. I just stopped by to make sure Nick got back all right and . . . " He hesitated and jingled the car keys in his pocket. "And to see if Nick needs a ride to Preston Monday morning."

"No, I'll give her a ride," Richard spoke up, smiling at Nick. "I'm not doing anything Monday morning. I'd love to go for a little drive and see where you're working."

Nick's cheeks were a deep pink and her eyes betrayed her embarrassment. "You don't need to make a special trip, Richard, because . . . "

"Don't worry about it," Richard came back cheerily. "I'd love to drive you to Preston."

"No problem," Aaron said, forcing himself to smile and moving toward the door. "I'll catch you all later."

Aaron's cheeks burned all the way home as he painfully relived the awkwardness of his barging in on Nick's reunion with Richard.

"That was quick," Regina said as he came into the house.

"Why didn't you tell me Richard Robbins was home?" he asked, angrily.

"I didn't know he was. I knew he was coming soon. Was he there?"

"Yeah, he was there," Aaron muttered, dropping on the sofa. "I walked right in expecting to . . . " He shook his head. "I felt like a jerk. Richard was the only one there who wasn't aware that Nick and I have been dating."

"Hasn't Nick talked to you about Richard?"

"Sure. We've talked." He shook his head. "I guess I just expected him to stay in the mission field." He studied Regina as she sat across the room from him in a glide-rocker. "Was Nick pretty thick with Richard before he left?"

She thought a moment before answering. "I suppose," she said slowly. "I think everyone in the ward thought they were right for each other, and I guess we all assumed she was going to marry him." She shrugged. "With a lot of girls you just know they're not going to wait around for a missionary. You know they're going to be married or engaged by the time the missionary gets home." She shook her head. "I didn't ever think that of Nick and Richard."

"You never told me that."

"Well, when you and Nick hit it off the way you did, I suppose I stopped thinking of Richard."

"Nick has talked about Richard, but I've always had the impression he was more her brothers' idea."

"It's been a while since I've talked to her about him, but I know she was writing pretty steadily to him at one time."

"Nick didn't ever hide that from me. Maybe she hasn't hidden anything from me. Maybe I just haven't been listening or seeing."

"You like her, don't you?" Regina asked gently.

Aaron took a deep breath and exhaled slowly. "I like her. I didn't know how much until I made that drive from Preston to here alone. I thought of Nick the whole while. That's why I didn't waste any time in getting over there. I was really looking forward to seeing her. I didn't expect her to be sitting next to Richard Robbins with his hand on her knee while he talked about Japan."

Aaron slumped down on the sofa and leaned his head back, staring up at the ceiling. After a few moments he said, "Regina, I saw AJ."

"Daddy?"

Aaron nodded and explained briefly what had happened. "He wasn't like I expected. He seems . . . " Aaron thought for a long time before continuing. "I don't know how he seems. Just a lot different from what I had expected. He's an old man."

"The last seventeen years haven't been easy for Daddy. He's sick. I don't know with what. He won't say."

"I felt sorry for him. I didn't think I'd ever say that."

"Will you see him again?"

Aaron put his hands behind his head and closed his eyes momentarily. "Part of me says no."

"And the other part of you?"

"The other part . . . Well, that part is a bit curious. My past is a puzzle. Some of the pieces are missing."

"And maybe Daddy can help you find those missing pieces?"

He sat up, leaned forward, and rested his forearms on his knees. "How does Mom feel about AJ?"

"Mom's happy with Jack. It hurt Mom when Daddy left. More than either one of us will ever know. But she's forgiven Daddy. A long time ago."

On Monday morning Aaron drove by Nick several times as she manned her flag station on the highway. Each time he waved. Nick smiled and seemed herself, but Aaron couldn't get his mind off Friday evening when Nick had been sitting next to Richard with his hand on her knee. When the crew broke for lunch, Aaron ate in his truck, so he wouldn't run into Nick.

After work, Aaron locked up his truck and climbed down to the ground.

"You've managed to keep yourself busy today."

Aaron turned. Nick stood a few feet away hugging her hard hat in front of her. "It's been one of those days," he said sheepishly, dusting at his pants with his hands.

"Saturday morning I got up early and went out for a run. I thought I needed some good thinking time. I do my best thinking when I run. I discovered something."

Aaron studied her. "What's that?"

"I'm out of shape. By the time I finished my five miles, my tongue was hanging down to my knees. My coach hasn't been pushing me much since we moved up north here."

"I'll give you a ride back to town, and we'll get out and hit the pavement."

The ride back to town and their jog together were both quiet occasions. At the end of their five-mile run, Nick walked off the stiffness in her legs and caught her breath. Aaron walked quietly beside her.

"I'm sorry about Friday night. Richard was waiting for me at Aunt Marge's after work. I wasn't sure how long you were going to be, so I caught a ride home with him. Aunt Marge did tell you, didn't she?"

"She said an old family friend had taken you home."

"I'm sorry."

There was a pause. Then Aaron remarked casually, "Experience indicates that three's a crowd." Nick continued walking without responding. "How do you feel about him?"

"Aaron, I'm not sure I've been honest with you. Maybe it's more that I haven't been completely honest with myself." Aaron didn't speak, waiting for her to explain. "Richard and I have been good friends for a long time. I know the boys have kind of figured out in their minds that Richard and I would . . . well, someday tie the knot. I've resented that. I suppose that's the thing that I've emphasized most with you. What I haven't admitted more openly to you, or even to myself, is that in spite of the pressure put on me by my brothers, I have always liked Richard."

"And I was just kind of a stand-in until he came back?"

Nick stopped, faced Aaron, and took his hand. "No, that isn't what I mean. Everything that's happened between you and me has been real. Being with you these past weeks has been wonderful. I wouldn't want to change any of that."

"But you have some memories of Richard you wouldn't

want to change either. And you've had some feelings for Richard that you haven't felt for me. Is that it?"

She hesitated and then nodded slowly. "Yes. Seeing Richard this weekend has made me do some serious thinking. That's why I wanted to jog on Saturday morning. I needed time to think."

"Does Richard know about us? Or am I just an 'old family friend'?"

"Last night I told Richard about you."

Aaron pulled his hand free and turned away, taking several steps away from Nick.

"So are you still interested in having a running coach?" he asked.

She smiled and nodded.

"Is that your only interest in me now? Do you want me to be *just* your running coach?"

"I'm not sure right now. Can you understand that?"

"I don't know. Putting it bluntly, I'm not sure I can be content with being just your coach. I guess I've been a player-coach too long to go back to the other."

Nick walked over to him, took his arm, and started walking toward Marge's place. "I don't know if I'd want you as just a coach. I'm not sure I know what I want. I know that I don't want you to just walk away without looking back."

"But you don't want Richard to walk away either."

"I guess I need time to think, without pressure from anyone. Is that being selfish?"

Aaron smiled. "Well, for right now maybe we've got it all figured out. I've got you in Preston. Richard can make his play when you're in Bear River. But not without a little competition, though. By the time this job is done, maybe you won't be so confused."

During the next four days things seemed to return to normal. After work on Thursday, Aaron and Nick went jogging. Then Aaron returned to his motel room to clean up. He and Nick hadn't made any specific plans, but he did want to see her that evening. After he'd eaten dinner, he pulled up in front of Marge's place. There was a Buick with Utah plates parked in front. An uneasy foreboding tightened in the pit of his stomach.

Marge greeted him happily. "Hello, Aaron, come on in."

Nick was in the living room, sitting in the overstuffed chair while Richard sat across the room on the couch. Both Nick and Richard stood when Aaron entered. "You two have met," Nick said, blushing brightly and looking from one to the other. Turning to Aaron, she added, "Richard drove up. It was a complete surprise. He wants to take me out to dinner." She bit down on her lower lip. "Would you like to come? The three of us could go together."

Aaron glanced at Richard, who didn't look as though that's what he would have suggested.

"Well, actually, I just ate. I'll pass tonight. Thanks."

He turned to leave. Nick followed him out to the front walk. "I didn't know he was coming," she said, touching his arm.

He turned to her and smiled wryly. "I assumed Preston was my territory. I guess I was wrong."

"Aaron, I don't want this to change anything."

Aaron smiled, though it hurt. "Have a nice dinner, Nick. I'd like to drive you home tomorrow."

"It's a date."

"Tell Richard if he drives up Friday for you, it's a wasted trip."

Nick smiled. "I'll tell him."

Chapter Seventeen

"Aaron Solinski?" the voice called from behind Aaron as he walked toward his motel room door after leaving Nick and Richard. Aaron turned and saw a man in a suit approach with his hand extended. "Aaron, I'm Bishop Tucker. Maybe you don't remember me."

"Sure, Bishop, I remember."

"Can we talk?"

"Is my room all right?"

Bishop Tucker nodded and followed Aaron into his room. Aaron pulled up a chair for the bishop and then sat down on the edge of the bed.

Bishop Tucker was in his middle fifties. He had close-clipped, reddish blond hair that was combed straight back. A sprinkle of faint freckles peppered a face that was a bit rough and unpolished. He had clear, piercing blue eyes that exuded warmth as well as determination.

The bishop looked down at his clasped hands and then he shifted his weight and turned his penetrating gaze on Aaron. "I came to visit with you about your father."

"You mean AJ?"

The bishop studied Aaron for a moment and nodded. He picked at a couple of specks of lint on his pant legs and pursed his lips. "I'm not sure where to begin." He cleared his throat. "Maybe I need to just talk from my heart."

"I'm listening."

"Do you mind if I tell you something about your father and me?" Aaron shrugged slightly. Bishop Tucker leaned back in his chair and crossed his legs. "AJ came to me about three years ago. I hadn't been serving as bishop for more than two weeks when he came to my home. He was drunk that day, had been for about a week straight. I hadn't seen AJ for nearly twenty years. I didn't recognize him. The last time I had seen AJ, he was working for Motorola. If I'm not mistaken, you were about five or six then."

The bishop stopped speaking and swallowed as a wave of sudden emotion washed over him. Tears sparkled in his eyes. He blinked them away and then reached into his back pocket for a handkerchief. Wiping his eyes, he cleared his throat and continued. "I first met AJ in Mexico. He was my senior companion. I had just informed the mission president that I was going home. He had tried to talk me out of it, but I'd made up my mind. I didn't know the language, I couldn't stand the food, I was homesick, and I had a girlfriend at home waiting for me. The president finally told me he'd let me go if I'd just spend two weeks working with an Elder Tippets."

Bishop Tucker smiled. "Well, you can probably guess how that story ended. Elder Tippets and I eventually served that same mission president as his two assistants. Elder Tippets left Mexico before me. I put him on the plane for home. And cried like a baby. He had saved my life."

"He ruined mine, Bishop," Aaron injected simply, with little emotion.

Bishop Tucker nodded without responding verbally to Aaron's remark. "For three years I've been more than an old friend to AJ. I've been his bishop. He's tormented by the horrible damage he has done to you and so many others.

"Not once in the time that he has been here in Preston has he ever made an excuse for himself. He accepts the blame for his mistakes. You're probably aware that he was excommunicated years ago. He would like to return to the Church. AJ's been through a disciplinary council with the stake president. He could be rebaptized. He hasn't been."

"Maybe he has further to go than you thought."

"Perhaps." Bishop Tucker blew his nose and then studied Aaron for a moment before continuing. "Do you know how AJ spends his time?" Aaron didn't answer. He returned Bishop Tucker's gaze, unmoved. "There are widows in Preston who have received help from AJ and who think of him as the kindest, most charitable man they know. They don't know his past—only his quiet, simple acts of Christian service. If someone's car breaks down on the highway, AJ stops. It has become a habit with him. Do you know why he does that?"

The bishop waited for Aaron to answer. Aaron remained stoically silent. "AJ feels unworthy to do anything but serve others. He told me the other day that the only time he feels released from his guilt is when he's doing something for somebody else. He said that perhaps after he has served enough, he will feel worthy to rejoin the Church."

"What does this have to do with me?" Aaron questioned.

"He needs you, Aaron."

"I needed him once." Aaron swallowed, fighting back a sudden emotion welling up inside him. "He wasn't there. Bishop, do you have any idea how hard it is for a nine-year-old kid to understand why his father would just walk out of his life?" Bishop Tucker didn't answer. "Did he ask you to talk to me?"

The bishop shook his head. "The day he first saw you here in Preston, he came to me. He cried like a child. His greatest fear is that you will never feel that you can forgive him. He doesn't blame you for resenting him for what he did. In fact, he feels you're right. He doesn't feel he has the right to even ask you for forgiveness."

"Maybe he's right."

"I hope not."

Aaron pushed himself up from the bed, walked to the window, pulled back the drapes, and peered out into the darkness. "What are you asking me?"

"Your father is dying."

Aaron turned and faced the bishop. "How?"

"The doctors thought it was leukemia at first."

"And now?"

"They're not sure. And AJ won't go back to be tested. He says he's a dead man either way. He'd rather not know."

Aaron swallowed and wet his lips. "AIDS?"

Bishop Tucker hesitated. "I suppose there's a possibility."

The muscles along Aaron's jaw tightened. "Did he stoop to that, too?"

"Not what you're thinking. But he didn't lead a good life. After he left your mother, he remarried. That didn't last. A short while later he married again. She left him for a younger guy. That's when things really took a nosedive for AJ. He was drinking heavily by then. He couldn't hold a job. He went from one relationship to another. Five years ago he married for a fourth time. She was an alcoholic. By then, so was he. Three years ago they were traveling together and rolled the car. He was buckled in. She wasn't.

"It was after her funeral that he came here, knowing he had to either claw his way out of the dismal abyss he'd dropped into or end his miserable life."

"How long does he have to live?" There was a shade of compassion in the question, the first that Aaron had showed.

"A few months. A year." Bishop Tucker shook his head. "The last six months or so he's looked better. But he doesn't have long."

"I don't see that there is anything I can do."

"If you want AJ out of your life, that will come soon enough. But don't let him die without allowing him to make peace with you."

Long after Bishop Tucker left, Aaron lay on his bed staring up at the ceiling. In the morning when he awoke, he was still in his clothes and the lamp next to the bed was still on.

"I missed you last night," Nick commented as the two drove toward Bear River the following evening.

"Richard didn't look too excited about having a tagalong. Even 'an old family friend.'"

Nick leaned back in her seat, reached over, and tugged playfully on Aaron's earlobe. "I was in the mood to see an old friend of the family," she said quietly.

They drove in silence for a moment; then Aaron spoke. "Would you do me a favor next week when we come back up to Preston?"

"Sure. What is it?"

"I'd like you to go with me to see . . . AJ."

Nick straightened up. "I'd love to. He wants to see you."

"How do you know?"

"I've gone over there a couple of times. And talked."

"To AJ?"

Nick nodded and smiled. "I don't spend all my time with old family friends. In fact, I promised him yesterday that I would take him some supper Monday evening. We can both go over."

Aaron stared at her a moment and then shook his head. "I've spent the biggest part of my life trying to despise AJ and yet forget him at the same time. Here I've come face-to-face with him. Maybe I'm as wrong now as he was seventeen years ago."

* * * * *

Nick spent that weekend with Richard Robbins at his family reunion in Salt Lake. Aaron spent all day Saturday working in Regina's yard. And thinking of AJ. His mind kept returning to his conversation with Bishop Tucker. He couldn't shake the feeling that the AJ in Preston was not the same AJ that he had once learned to hate.

Monday evening Aaron was a bit nervous as he helped Nick carry hot stew, fresh baked bread, and a green salad from the car to AJ's porch. Aaron knocked on the screen door.

"I'll be right there, young lady," AJ called from inside. "I was just putting a . . . " The words died in his throat as he hurried into the living room and saw Aaron standing at the door with Nick at his side. He wiped his hands on his pant legs and raked through his hair with his fingers. "Come in," he invited, just above a whisper.

"Hello, Mr. Tippets," Nick called out cheerfully. "I hope you're hungry."

"I'm always hungry for good food."

There was plenty of food, and since Aaron and Nick hadn't eaten, AJ set two more places and insisted they stay and eat with him. Had it not been for Nick's happy, casual conversation, though, the meal would have been eaten in silence.

"Well, that was mighty good," AJ commented, wiping his mouth with a paper napkin. "I don't get cooking like that very often." He looked at Aaron and Nick and smiled. "Now it's my turn. Old bachelors generally don't make very good cooks, and I'm no exception." He grinned. "One of these days I'll probably poison myself, but I can throw together a pretty decent Mexican meal. Come over tomorrow."

Aaron was about to protest, but Nick gripped his hand

under the table and spoke up, "We'd love to. It's been months since I've had some good Mexican food."

"Is seven o'clock too late?"

"Seven is fine," Nick said.

Tuesday evening Nick and Aaron returned to AJ's place. AJ greeted them at the door wearing a bright red apron. He was excited and happy to see them. "You won't believe this," he grinned proudly, "but the food's even ready."

"It better be," Nick joked. "I'm starved."

"I just hope it's good," AJ replied a bit nervously.

"So do I," Nick came back seriously, and then grinned.

The food was not only authentic but delicious. AJ had fixed chicken enchiladas, refried beans, and Spanish rice. There were plenty of tortilla chips, salsa, and ice cold root beer. The two men were a bit reticent at first, but Nick's cheerful compliments and playful banter eventually dispelled the tension between the father and son. By the time they were finished eating, the three of them were visiting and joking freely.

After the dishes were cleared, the three of them sat around the table and talked. AJ was interested in everything that Aaron had been doing, so with some gentle but persistent prodding from Nick, he spoke of his mission in Peru, his years at college and law school, and his summer work experiences. It was almost ten before anyone really noticed the time.

"We'd better start on these dishes," Nick said, standing up, "and then get out of here. Aaron and I will be falling asleep on the job tomorrow."

"I'll do the dishes," AJ said, pushing back his chair and standing. "You two run on."

Although Nick and Aaron both offered to help, AJ wouldn't hear of it. Pushing them to the door, he said, "This was my treat. It would ruin things if you stayed and cleaned up. Now get out of here," he added, trying to sound stern. "I've done dishes before."

AJ followed them out to the car. "You're welcome back any time. You don't have to wait for anything special. Just stop by. As they used to say in Mexico, '*Estan en su casa.*'"

"Well, if I'm not mistaken," Nick spoke up, "I believe it's somebody else's turn to fix the food." Aaron flinched as Nick jabbed him with a finger.

"Is that a hint?" Aaron questioned, laughing.

"He's not very quick," Nick commented to AJ, nodding toward Aaron, "but he catches on fairly well if you get downright blunt with him."

"I guess I could arrange for supper one of these evenings," Aaron announced. "I'm not much of a cook, but I can order a decent pizza."

"Let me buy the pizza," AJ spoke up. "You pick out what you want, and I'll—"

Aaron laughed and shook his head. "No, it's my turn." He gave Nick a playful push. "I don't want anybody accusing me of not pulling my own weight."

Nick and Aaron were quiet for the first minute or so as they drove away from AJ's place. Nick was the one to break the silence. "We need to visit him again, Aaron. Soon." Aaron didn't say anything. "He loves having you there. He can't take his eyes off you, and he hangs on your every word."

"It's easier than I figured," Aaron said quietly. "I mean easier to be there than I thought it would be."

"We will go back, won't we?"

Aaron smiled over at her. "You'd think he was *your* dad." He took a quick breath and exhaled immediately. "You'll go with me?"

"You know I will." She smiled. "Does that mean we're on for pizza tomorrow night?"

"You're not the least bit pushy, are you?" Aaron joked.

"Only when I need to be," she said coyly.

The next evening AJ had the table set with plates, glasses, and silverware. "Pizza's supposed to be a no-mess operation," Aaron commented when he saw the table. "I figured we'd eat with our fingers. Then there'd be no cleanup."

"I wanted it to be nice," AJ replied, his cheeks coloring.

As they finished the last of the food, AJ spoke. "I should have picked up a half gallon of ice cream." He laughed. "I know someone here who loves rocky road ice cream." He grinned over at Aaron. Looking at Nick, he added, nodding to Aaron, "Wart here could put away piles of rocky road ice cream."

"Wart?" Nick asked, laughing.

AJ smiled and shook his head. "I always called him Wart. You remember that?" he asked, turning to Aaron. Aaron smiled wanly and nodded. "I'll bet you haven't been called Wart for a long time, have you?" He looked down at the tabletop and covered his eyes with his hand. AJ's tears were entirely unexpected.

Nick and Aaron sat in uncomfortable silence until the old man was able to compose himself. He wiped his eyes with his napkin. "I'm sorry. I didn't mean to do that. I wanted this to be a happy time." Taking a deep breath and trying to smile, he said, "I'd like to get that ice cream, though. I can run down to the store and be back in no time." He was on his feet and to the door before the other two could protest.

Later, after the ice cream had been eaten, Nick started to clear the table. AJ was on his feet immediately, refusing the help. "I'll get it, young lady. If someone else brings in the food, then I can sure clean up."

"It's no trouble."

"I insist."

As AJ cleared, he spoke to Aaron. "Staying down in that old motel room can't be very homey." He had his back to Aaron and was rinsing dishes in the sink. "I mean a motel room's all right for a night or two, but after that it gets pretty stale. I've got plenty of room here. Just going to waste. You ought to stay here. I wouldn't bother you."

The offer took Aaron completely by surprise. He glanced in Nick's direction. She pleaded with her eyes and nodded her head, mouthing the word yes. Bishop Tucker's words came back to him.

"I'd understand if you'd rather not," AJ went on when the offer wasn't accepted immediately. "I know I'm not the—"

"That would be fine," Aaron cut in.

"You could move over tomorrow," AJ said, turning around, his hands dripping soapy water on the floor. "I'll help you."

"I don't have much. I'll drop by after work."

AJ turned back to the sink. "Thanks, Wart. Thanks."

After Aaron and Nick had said their good nights to AJ and were walking out to the car, Nick whispered, her voice breaking, "Thanks, Aaron. I was praying you wouldn't turn him down."

The next afternoon Aaron moved in with AJ. AJ had a room fixed for him and fried Spam and potatoes for his dinner. "I don't get fancy," AJ apologized as he piled the potatoes and Spam on Aaron's plate, "but there's always plenty. I can open another can of meat if you'd like."

They ate their meal in awkward silence. Without Nick

there the conversation didn't come as easily. "It was good," Aaron commented, pushing back from the table and starting to clear.

"No!" AJ burst out. "Definitely not!"

"Last night you said if someone fixed the meal, you'd do the dishes," Aaron said lightly. "You cooked; I'll clean."

"Maybe another time," AJ pleaded, grabbing for the plate in Aaron's hand. "Tonight, let me clean up. Go see Nick." He shook his head. "Now that's one special little lady."

Aaron smiled. "Unfortunately, I'm not the only caller."

"Then don't sit around with an old man. Go after her."

A dim light still burned in the front window when Aaron returned to AJ's place at eleven. When he entered, he found AJ asleep in the overstuffed chair with an open book in his lap. Aaron touched his shoulder and the older man stirred. "You didn't have to wait up for me." Aaron smiled.

"You're back," AJ said, blinking and rubbing his eyes.

"You should have gone to bed."

"I *wanted* to wait up for you," he answered. "I haven't ever had that chance." Aaron looked away. Stepping to the sofa, he sat down.

A long silence ensued, both men staring down at the floor.

"How long have you been doing these odd jobs and things?" Aaron finally asked, wanting to break the uncomfortable silence. "You used to make pretty good money as an engineer."

AJ frowned and pulled the hair on the back of his neck. "I've done a lot of dumb things. Leaving your mother and you kids was the worst. But not the only one. Without going into detail, I guess the easiest way to explain it is that a drunk makes a mighty poor engineer. I started doing odd jobs because I could only manage to stay sober for a few days, at least sober enough to fix a washer or a dryer or dig a trench for a sewer line. Actually, I really haven't minded doing that sort of thing." AJ studied Aaron, who stared back at his father. "I know what you're thinking. An educated guy like me should be off doing great things instead of running around doing common labor. You're probably right. But it's too late now to change all that."

"I was just wondering."

"Do you like this young woman?" AJ asked, anxious to change the direction of the conversation.

Smiling, Aaron nodded. "More each time I'm with her."

"This isn't the same one you were engaged to."

Aaron stared at AJ. "How'd you know about Brittany?"

"Oh, your mother has written off and on. She's tried to keep me informed." He cleared his throat. "Nick's different from that Brittany, isn't she?"

"Yeah, she's different."

"Don't let her slip away."

"I want to make sure she's the right one. I don't want to make a mistake."

AJ bowed his head. "Like your mother and I made. Is that it?" he questioned sadly.

"Well, I wasn't exactly saying that."

"Wart, . . . " His face flushed red. "I mean, Aaron. When your mother and I met and courted and decided to get married, we knew we were made for each other. There are few things I've known more surely than I knew that your mother was the right one for me. Your mother felt that, too. All of that was right. And good."

"But—"

"There's no *but*," AJ said, holding up his hand. "Back then we made the right decision. What happened later was my fault. Your mother and I had something beautiful and pure. I was the one who destroyed it. But destroying it with my foolishness and selfishness didn't change the fact that in the beginning it was all right and all good."

AJ held his head in his hands for a moment. "I wish I could go back and change all of that. I suppose I could live knowing I had destroyed *my* life. But it's the other lives that haunt me. I'm sorry for what I did to you and your sisters and your mother.

"I do want you to know one thing. Perhaps this will be the hardest thing for you to understand. I still love your mother. More than you or she will ever know. I know I can never go back. Jack has done for her what I should have done. He was the man I should have been. And because of that, he has what I gave away."

For several minutes the two sat there without speaking or looking at each other. Finally Aaron stood up. "I'd better get to bed. Six o'clock comes pretty early."

"Aaron," AJ called out as Aaron started down the hall, "thanks for coming over. This little dump isn't much, but it's like home again."

"Thanks for the invite."

Aaron picked Nick up just after five-thirty on Friday afternoon. "I'm glad Richard didn't make a wasted trip," Aaron laughed as he helped Nick into the Civic. "I've been looking forward to this little jaunt all week."

"So have I."

"What do you say we take the long way home?"

"The long way?"

"Around by Bear Lake and down Logan Canyon. It's a little longer, but the scenery is worth it."

"That sounds great. I'm in no hurry."

Aaron laughed. "Me either. Besides, that way I can keep you away from other old family friends a little longer."

They drove up past Mink Creek, around the mountain through Paris, St. Charles, Garden City, and the other small towns that crowded the shores of the beautiful, blue Bear Lake. As they finally left the valley and climbed to the summit before descending through Logan Canyon, Aaron pulled the Civic off the road. "How about taking a last look at Bear Lake from up here?"

The two left the car and walked up a round hill covered with grass and yellow wildflowers. Facing a gentle breeze blowing up from the lake, they gazed out over the valley with the deep blue of the lake shimmering below them. The sun was dropping behind the mountains to the west, casting gray shadows across the valley.

As Aaron held her hand, Nick turned and leaned against him. "This has been a wonderful week, Aaron." She bit down on her lip and looked into his face. "Thanks for including me."

Putting his arms around her, Aaron pulled her close and kissed her, first on the forehead and then on the lips. For several moments they held to that embrace. "Have you had enough time to think?" Aaron asked, smiling as they separated slightly.

"I have certainly enjoyed these moments of reflection. I'm not sure I want them to end."

"I guess that means you can tell Richard to get lost."

Nick slapped playfully at him. "Your sense of timing is atrocious, Solinski."

The sun had disappeared by the time they climbed into the Civic to continue their trip down Logan Canyon. They reached Bear River a few minutes before ten. Aaron helped Nick carry her things into the house.

"Well, where have you been?" Jared demanded angrily

as they pushed through the front door. "We've been calling all over."

Nick's mouth dropped open and she asked, "What do you mean?"

"It's ten o'clock. How long does it take you to drive home?"

"That was my fault," Aaron spoke up. "I took her on the scenic route by Bear Lake."

"We've been waiting dinner for you," Jared started again, ignoring Aaron's explanation. "I told you last Sunday we had a surprise for you."

"Jared, you didn't say anything about my being home at a certain time," Nick came back, losing some of her shocked surprise and defending herself.

"Richard's here. We were having a special dinner for him. We wanted you here."

Nick cast a quick glance at Aaron, who still stood in the doorway holding her suitcase. Joseph and Joshua came into the living room from the kitchen. James and Jacob, followed by Richard Robbins, made their solemn entrance. The boys' irritation was evident as they all glowered at Aaron.

"It looks like I'm making a habit of busting up family gatherings," Aaron mumbled.

"You're right there," Jared snapped. "The least you could have done is give us a call."

"Jared, you don't have any cause to jump all over Aaron," Nick spoke up. "I was the one who should have called. And if you had plans for the evening, then you should have explained what they were."

"All I asked you to do was watch after her," Jared bristled, turning on Aaron. "I wasn't planning on you moving in and setting up house."

"Watch after me?"

"That's why he started hanging around," Jared fired off.

"I asked him to take you out a few times. This whole mess is my fault."

"What are you talking about?" Nick demanded.

"He was doing *me* a favor when he took you out."

"Don't you ever get tired of trying to run my life?"

"I get tired of him butting into it," Jared snapped back, jabbing a finger in Aaron's direction.

"I don't remember asking anyone to look out for me. I didn't ask for anyone to throw a surprise party. And I certainly don't need you to give me the third degree as soon as I walk through the door."

Snatching her suitcase from Aaron, she stomped out of the living room and down the hall to her room without saying another word. Everyone was silent for a moment. Finally Jared turned to Aaron and said, "I don't think Nick's in the mood to visit with you any more tonight."

"I think I have a right to explain some things to Nick," Aaron came back. "I didn't ask your sister out because of anything you said. Your idea stunk from the beginning."

"I'll let Nick know you said so."

"I'd feel better telling her myself."

"Tonight you'll have to let me relay your message."

"She's not old enough to speak for herself?"

"She's just not in the mood."

"She isn't? Or you're not?"

"Good night, Solinski. It's time you left."

Chapter Eighteen

"The phone's for you," Regina said, holding out the phone to her brother Sunday evening.

"Aaron, Jared Jerard here. I'm calling to let you know that Nick won't need a ride to Preston in the morning."

Aaron didn't respond immediately. He hadn't seen Nick since Friday night. She hadn't been in church that morning, and twice, when he had stopped by her house on Saturday, she had been gone. "Is something wrong?"

"No," Jared came back casually, "she just won't need a ride."

"Can I speak to her?"

"She went to bed early. She's been feeling rotten all day."

"Well, tell her to take care of herself."

Monday morning when Aaron drove his dump truck past the spot where Nick usually directed traffic, a replacement was there. At noon Aaron found the girl who had taken Nick's place. "You're new here."

The girl was eating her lunch with three of the crew members. She nodded her head and smiled.

"What happened to Nick Jerard?"

She shrugged. "All I know is I got a call last night and was told to be up here this morning to finish out this job."

After work Aaron stopped by Marge's place. "Do you know where Nick is?"

"Her brother called last night and said she'd decided to stay in Bear River and go back to work in the Overson office in Tremonton. Didn't she say something to you?"

Aaron shook his head. "You didn't talk to her, Mrs. Eaton?"

"Jared said she wasn't feeling well and had gone to bed. James drove up this morning to pick up her things."

Monday night was a quiet, lonely one for Aaron. AJ was gone, helping a family with some plumbing problems that had developed late in the afternoon. Aaron fixed some sandwiches, poured himself a glass of milk, and ate in the living room.

AJ didn't have a phone or Aaron might have called Nick. Instead he was left with his own thoughts, to worry and speculate about the events of the last three days. After a while, frustrated with his own company, he began in the kitchen and started cleaning the house. Staying active helped keep his mind off Nick.

He lost track of time and was surprised when he heard AJ's Dodge pull up in front. He looked at his watch. It was nearly midnight.

"Hey, what happened here?" he heard AJ exclaim as he pulled open the screen door, stepped inside, and let it bang shut behind him. "What've you been doing, Wart?"

"I decided to clean the place up," Aaron answered, entering the living room. "Once I got started, I didn't know how to quit. Do you always work till midnight?"

AJ shook his head. "No. But either I worked, or the Montes family went without water till tomorrow." He looked around. "I've never seen this place look this good. Did Nick help you?"

"No. Nick's not working up here anymore."

"What happened?"

"Hey, I was thinking," Aaron spoke up, changing the

subject, "with some paint we could do a real job on the outside of this place. The inside could use some too."

"I didn't invite you over here to put you to work. I
thought you could relax and enjoy yourself."

Aaron smiled wanly. "I'm going to have a little time on
my hands. I'd kind of like to keep busy."

AJ looked around. "I have let the place go to seed. I'm
game if you are."

The next day after work, Aaron found AJ already scrap-
ing paint off the exterior of the house. Aaron joined him.
They worked until dark, then AJ took Aaron down to
Big J's Drive-in for a cheeseburger and fries.

"I think we can start painting tomorrow," AJ observed
as he bit down into his cheeseburger and reached for a napkin to wipe his mouth. "I'll pick the paint up in the afternoon. Is blue still a favorite color of yours?"

"Yeah. How'd you remember that?"

AJ chewed slowly. Swallowing, he ran his tongue around
in his mouth and across his lips. "I remember a lot of things,
Wart." He pressed his lips together. "That's the hard part. I
gave away so much for so little. And I'm always remembering. Wart, I wish I could make up for . . . " He swallowed
and shrugged helplessly. "For everything."

"Tell me something. Just give it to me straight. All
right?" AJ stared at his son and nodded, somewhat fearfully.
"During all those years did you think of us? Did you think of
me?"

After a long pause AJ spoke. "I won't go into the details
of the early years. But when I left with Linda," he added in
a pained voice, "I rationalized that I needed her more than I
needed anything else. Sometime later I realized how wrong
I was."

AJ pushed his food aside and clasped his hands in front
of him on the table. "By the time my mind cleared some,

your mother was already married to Jack, and there was no going back. Then when your mom and Jack contacted me and asked if Jack could adopt you . . . Well, my first reaction was an emphatic no. I was going to make everything up to you. I was going to go back and repair the damage. But Linda and I were going through our divorce and I . . . " AJ coughed uncomfortably. "And I was mixed up with another gal. That didn't work out, either."

AJ gnawed on his lower lip. In the fluorescent lighting of the restaurant, his face looked grizzled and thin. Aaron found it painful to look at him as the old man struggled to explain his behavior.

"Well, after more careful thinking I realized that I would never be able to make things up to you the way you deserved. I realized—and this was the part that hurt the most—that Jack was in a better position to fill the void than I was. If I had tried to come back into your life, it would have just started up a tug-of-war between your mom and me. And you would have been the unwilling rope in the middle. You can call that a cop-out, a chicken's move, or whatever you like, but I figured I was doing what was best for you."

AJ stared across the table at Aaron. "I gave my consent to Jack and your mother. I told her that I would stay out of your life until you were eighteen if she would just stay in contact with me and let me know what you were doing. I kept my word. Not because it was easy. You might not believe this, but I gave Jack permission to adopt you because I knew that under the circumstances he could do more for you than I could."

"I turned eighteen a few years ago. About eight."

AJ averted his eyes and nodded. "I know. But my life was a mess then. You might figure it's not a lot better now, but it is."

Aaron played absentmindedly with a half dozen cold

French fries in front of him. "Well, I appreciate you telling me."

The next day after work, Aaron and AJ began painting the house. They started late each afternoon and worked into the night, rigging up a system of outside lights so they could continue. Friday evening they finished.

"I say tomorrow we get the inside," Aaron said, stepping back and admiring their work. "If we move everything out tonight, we can start early in the morning and keep going till we're done."

AJ flashed a tired grin. "If you're up to it, I am."

Even before the sun was up, AJ and Aaron were painting the inside of the small house. By evening they finished. As the sun was setting, they began moving the furniture from the front yard back into the house.

Sunday morning Aaron got up to go to church. AJ stayed in bed. "I better not try it today," he explained weakly to Aaron. "I think I pushed myself a little too far these last few days. But I'm glad I did."

Aaron looked down at AJ. His father's face was drawn and thin. Under the singlebed sheet he looked older and weaker than Aaron had seen him. "Maybe I'd better call a doctor."

AJ shook his head. "No, I'll be all right. I don't have anything a doctor can help me with."

"What *do* you have?"

AJ looked up from his pillow and smiled weakly. "It doesn't matter any more. I think it already has my number."

"I can stay with you."

AJ shook his head. "No, you go to church. I've been sick before. I'll be all right."

By Sunday evening AJ was feeling a little better. The two of them went out under the shade of the trees and relaxed as a late afternoon breeze stirred the leaves and freshened what had been a hot, sultry day.

"Bishop Tucker asked about you today."

"Did you tell him that I'd be up and going by tonight?"

"He thinks you ought to see a doctor."

AJ chuckled. "All a doctor's going to do is take my money. And maybe prescribe something that's going to make me feel lots worse than I do right now."

"Bishop Tucker also said something about setting a baptism date."

AJ didn't respond for a moment. "Would you feel all right about that?" the old man asked.

"You're the one who would have to answer that. That's a personal matter between you and Bishop Tucker."

"But would you resent me coming back?"

Aaron thought for a moment. "I don't know. I don't know that it has anything to do with me."

AJ bowed his head in silent contemplation. After a few minutes, he lifted his head and turned to Aaron. "Son, in my bedroom on the top shelf of my closet there's a brown, metal box. Would you mind bringing it to me?"

Aaron found the box, brought it outside, and handed it to AJ. AJ fumbled with the metal clasp that held it shut and finally opened the box. Reaching in, he pulled out a bundle of money held together by a thick rubberband. He studied the packet for a moment and then held it out to Aaron.

"What's this for?" Aaron questioned, surprised. He stared at the money without taking it.

"I've saved a little money the last few years. Not much." He tossed the money into Aaron's lap. "There's almost thirteen hundred dollars there. I want you to have it."

For a long time Aaron didn't speak. Then he picked up the packet of bills and tapped it on the back of his hand.

Finally he took a deep breath and muttered, "AJ, I can't take your money."

"It's *your* money. That's why I saved it." Aaron studied AJ, his eyes questioning. "Back when your mother told me you were going to law school, I wanted to give you a hand. I hadn't done anything to help with your college, your mission, or anything else. Paying for your law school was something I wanted to do. I was hoping I'd have enough so I could cover all the costs." He shook his head. "Thirteen hundred dollars won't go too far. I don't know if it will even pay for one semester of law school. Probably won't. But I want you to have it."

Aaron shook his head and reached to hand the money back. "I can't take your money—money you're going to need."

AJ winced, but didn't take the proffered bills. "Aaron, I was going to give it to your mother and let her give it to you. But then when you came . . ." He ran his tongue over his lips. "I'd take it as a great favor if you'd accept it. I'd like to feel that in some little way I've done something. I know it's not much, and I'm seventeen years late, but I'd sure take it as a gesture of kindness if you'd accept this small donation for your schooling."

Aaron debated for a long time, still holding the money out for AJ to take. "Thanks, AJ," he finally said quietly, setting the money in his lap. "If you change your mind, I can—"

"No, it's yours. I want you to have it."

Another prolonged silence ensued. AJ was the first to speak again. "You know, son, I've wished I could give you more than money. Sometimes a father doesn't have material things to give his son. Sometimes the only thing he has to give a son is his good name. Sometimes a good name is worth more than anything." He shook his head. "I've felt awkward this past week. I've enjoyed having you here. It brings back so many memories. And a lot of hurt. Jack's a lucky man. He deserves to have a son like you. Although it does pain me to know that you're Aaron Solinski now." He cleared his throat and rubbed his hands up and down his thighs. "Do you ever think of yourself as Tippets any more?"

"Not for the past thirteen years."

AJ pushed himself up from his chair and paced a moment on the grass. When he stopped, his back was to Aaron. "Aaron, I don't know how much longer I'm going to be around. Probably not long. Although I really don't have the right to, I would ask one favor."

"Don't, AJ," Aaron spoke up, cutting him off. His tone was kind but firm. He stood and turned his back to AJ. "I'd rather you didn't ask. I've been glad that I could spend these last few days with you. I say that in all honesty. I suppose I've come to understand you better. And I've had my own eyes opened. But I'm Jack Solinski's son. I didn't necessarily want it that way. There was a time when I would have given about anything to be AJ Tippets's son. When Jack adopted me, I made up my mind that I was always going to be Aaron Solinski." He faced AJ and held the money out to him. "There are some things that can't be bought, if that's what this is for."

"It isn't," AJ was quick to explain. "The money, like I said, is for your school. There are no strings attached. I wasn't asking you to . . . " He shook his head. "It doesn't matter," he said softly. "After everything that's happened, I guess there are some things I don't have a right to ask for."

Aaron turned and entered the house, leaving AJ alone as the shadows of evening fingered their way through the trees.

Chapter Nineteen

Wednesday afternoon Aaron had the Civic packed and was preparing to leave Preston. "I had hoped you'd stay longer," AJ said as he walked Aaron to the car.

"Well, they cut back two drivers. The biggest part of the job is over. I'll be heading back to Tempe in a bit, so the boss figured I was the natural one to cut. J. T. will let me work another week or so in the Tremonton yard, so it won't hurt me."

"And you'll be closer to that young lady of yours," AJ said, winking and smiling.

Aaron shook his head. "I don't know how she feels anymore."

"You should have been on the phone with her a few times instead of painting and fixing up this place."

"Oh, I thought about it. A lot. But I knew if I called, and she wasn't there, I'd start wondering if . . . "

"Don't just guess. Ask her."

"I'll be gone in a couple of weeks. Maybe it's just as well it end this way."

"You could always stick around this part of the country."

Aaron laughed. "And drive dump truck?"

"Well, I was talking to Ben Howard yesterday. He's the principal over at the high school. He said that one of his English teachers up and left. I told him you were an English teacher."

"I have a degree in English. I'm not sure I'd call myself an English teacher."

"He said he'd take you right now. It's not easy to get a teacher up here this close to the start of school."

"You're dreaming, AJ. My sail's already set. I'm on the way to becoming a lawyer. For better or for worse."

"Well, if you change your mind, you remember that you've got a place right here. After working as hard on this place as you did, I'd think you'd want to spend a little more time here."

Aaron studied the house. "The next thing you need to do is replace those shingles. The place will look new then."

"I'll save that project for when you come back."

Aaron nodded and held out his hand. "I better get going."

AJ gripped his hand tightly and looked into his eyes. He clamped his jaw tight to prevent his emotions from spilling over, but he was unable to shut off the tears. They sparkled in his eyes. "Good luck, Wart." He smiled. "Aaron. I guess I have no business calling a big, important, future lawyer Wart. It doesn't suit you any more." He swallowed hard. "If you don't get too busy, drop me a line."

"I'll do that."

As Aaron drove slowly from Preston, there was a dull ache in his chest and throat. He felt he should have said more to AJ, and yet he wasn't sure what more he could have said. At the edge of town, he pulled off the road and contemplated going back and trying one more time, but he discounted the idea after a moment, convinced that he wouldn't know any better the second time what to say or do than he had the first. A return would just be awkward, and perhaps painful, for both of them.

* * * * *

"What was it like being with Daddy?" Regina asked. She had finished putting in a load of laundry and came into the kitchen where Aaron was leaning against the counter, holding a handful of grapes.

He chewed pensively. "I guess I see things a lot differently than I did a few weeks ago. He's not the same guy I thought I hated. But it was a struggle. Some of those feelings festered a long time."

"Is he well?"

Aaron took a moment before answering. "Dad and AJ are the same age. But AJ looks older. Lots older. But he gets by." He heaved a sigh. "What's been happening around here?"

"I have some news for you." She avoided his eyes.

"What?"

"Brandon and I are . . . " She hesitated and pressed her lips together.

"You and Brandon have decided to bag the divorce and give marriage another try."

Regina nodded and smiled at her brother. "I've been excited to tell nearly everybody."

"Except me, is that it?"

She laughed nervously. "Yes. I wasn't sure how you'd feel about it."

Aaron shook his head and smiled ruefully. "Regina, if you feel good about Brandon, I'm not going to try to change your mind.

"I suppose I'll have to sort through a few of my feelings before I'll be able to forget what he's put you through. But it's not up to me. He'll probably want to boot me out of the house, won't he?"

"We didn't think we'd do anything until you returned to ASU."

"Oh, spare me, Regina," Aaron said, laughing and shaking his head. "If you two have made up your mind, don't hold off because of me. Call him and get him over here. I'll even help him move. If you make me."

"Well, actually, we planned to take a little trip together. Just the two of us, and then . . . "

"Kind of like a second honeymoon?"

"The first. We didn't have much of anything when we were married. We got married Friday night and spent the weekend getting our apartment ready. Monday morning we were both back in school. And that night Brandon had to work."

"Well, Regina, take your honeymoon now while you still have a live-in babysitter to help take care of the kids."

Regina pushed herself up from the chair, came around the table and over to Aaron. She put her arms around his neck and squeezed. "Thanks, Aaron. You don't know how much this all means to me." She released him and stepped back. "And I don't mean the babysitting part. Thanks for understanding."

"Well, that's why I came." He folded his arms across his chest and grinned. "Of course, I was expecting a different ending. But I'll settle for this. As long as you're happy."

"What about you and Nick?" Regina asked, returning to her chair at the table.

Aaron popped a couple of grapes into his mouth. "Who knows?"

"She's been wondering why you haven't called. I couldn't tell her anything. I didn't know."

"Why I didn't call *her*! After that Friday night? I just assumed Richard Robbins won out there."

"She wasn't with him Sunday. They were both at church, but I don't think they spoke to each other."

"Well, I thought . . . "

"I don't think you've been thinking very much, or you would have at least called her."

"But after that mess over at her place, and when she didn't return to Preston, it was like she didn't want to see me or be around me. Why would she do that if . . . "

"She works for Mr. Overson, not you. He's the one who told her to stay here. He said the office was a mess." She laughed. "He told her he wanted her doing something useful, not out taking flack from a bunch of disgruntled motorists."

"Jared made it sound like—"

"Aaron, Jared isn't Nick. He's tried to push Nick Richard's way. Nick doesn't push very easily. You should know that. She asked about you Sunday. She likes you, Aaron."

"She asked about me?" Regina nodded. "And what makes you think she still likes me?" he asked hopefully.

Regina smiled. "Just call it female intuition. She said she misses having you around to coach her. She said running isn't as exciting any more."

Setting his remaining grapes aside, Aaron glanced down at his watch. "She's probably out there now."

"So what are you doing here?"

"Can I borrow your bike?"

"Get out of here before I slap you for being so dense."

When Aaron reached the bridge, he leaned the bike against the cables and looked out across the river. The sun's reflection was blinding. Turning away, he looked up and down the road, hoping that he wasn't too late or that she hadn't decided not to run.

"I'm shaking like a fool," he muttered to himself, looking down at his hands. He smiled. "Someone would think I'd never met Nick in my life." He looked up and checked both banks. There was no one. Anxiously he paced along the cracked asphalt. Then trying to calm himself, he snatched up a few fragments of asphalt and began tossing them into the water.

He spotted her just as she started down the north bank on her return run. She didn't notice him until she reached the end of the bridge. She stopped, staring. Then, tentatively, she walked to the middle of the bridge where he was leaning against the steel cables.

Even with her face flushed and beaded with perspiration and her hair windblown and a bit limp, she was beautiful, Aaron thought. She wiped at her forehead with the back of her hand and stopped ten feet from where Aaron waited, her chest rising and falling as she struggled to catch her breath. They studied one another without speaking.

"I didn't know you were back," she finally spoke.

"J. T. booted me off the job. Told me I'd have to finish up in Tremonton."

"What are you doing here?" She nodded at the bridge, placing her hands on her hips and inhaling deeply.

Aaron considered the question, squinting into the glare on the river. "Just waiting for a perspiring maiden to jog by." He placed his hands on his hips. "You know, you used to be able to make that five-mile run in good time—without stopping here on the bridge to catch your breath. What you need is a hard-nosed coach to really push you."

"Do you have anybody in mind?"

"I could give you a few pointers. And I'd definitely push you."

Nick stared at him, her face solemnly guarded. Gradually, however, the somber mask relaxed and the makings of a smile pulled at the corners of her mouth and a lightness flickered in her dark eyes. "It's good to see you again, Coach."

Aaron stepped toward her. For a moment he looked at her and then reached out and took her hands.

"I'm all sweaty," she protested, tugging against his grasp.

"That's the least of my worries. I wasn't sure I was going to see you again. When you didn't return to Preston, I just—"

"Didn't Aunt Marge tell you anything?" she cut in.

"The only thing she said was that Jared had called and said you weren't coming back. After that Friday night, I assumed you were upset and didn't want to see me."

"I *was* upset. But not at you. At Jared. And everybody else who was trying to make me fit into their perfect little mold."

"Well, Richard was there and—"

"I told Richard that it was over."

"You're not still trying to decide?"

"After that last week in Preston, . . . I knew." She smiled and shrugged.

"Why didn't you call?"

Nick feigned an angry glare. "I'm still very traditional, Aaron Solinski. I don't call guys. Why didn't you call *me*?"

Aaron shook his head and grinned. "I guess because I'm a big fool. I don't know." Suddenly he pulled Nick to him, wrapping his arms around her and pressing his face into her damp hair. "Oh, Nick, I missed you. I don't know if there were five minutes during these last ten days that I didn't think of you, worrying about us, sure that I'd messed everything up and lost you."

Nick clung to him and buried her face against his neck and chest. "You're going to smell like a lathered workhorse," she said, half laughing and half crying.

Aaron held her tightly. "Coaches are used to a little perspiration."

"Good, because I don't want you to let go."

Aaron pulled away a little, put his hand under Nick's chin, lifted her face to his, and kissed her gently. "I love you, Nick," he whispered.

"I love you, Aaron."

They kissed again, standing there on the bridge, oblivious to everything around them. Still holding to each other, they separated slightly. "You know, every afternoon when I'd go jogging," Nick said, her voice husky and quavering, "and I'd cross the bridge, I'd remember how we used to stop here. And for the rest of my jog I'd cry, wondering if you'd ever be here again.

"This afternoon, before I reached the bridge, I told myself that I wasn't going to cry this time. I wasn't even going to look at this spot. And I didn't. But the whole time I ran, I was thinking of you. You'll think this is crazy, but I even dreamed of coming off the bank back there and seeing you. I knew I was just being stupid, and I told myself that I was going to run back across the bridge for home without even slowing down.

"And then when I came down the hill, there you were." She looked up at Aaron, her face inches from his. Her eyes were full of tears. Aaron gently brushed the tears away with his fingers. Then he touched her lips with his fingertips and smiled. "I found exactly what I came for." He kissed her again.

They stayed on the bridge, holding each other and talking, not wanting to separate. Aaron told of his time with AJ, how he had helped him fix up and paint his place, how he had come to better understand AJ and, at the same time, himself.

"Did you baptize him before you left?" Nick wondered.

The question took Aaron by surprise. "Why do you ask that? I mean, AJ mentioned baptism while I was there, and

Bishop Tucker told me that he had been cleared for rebaptism, but—"

"Oh, Aaron," Nick pleaded, "he's waiting for you to do it."

"Me?" Aaron stepped away from Nick. "Why *me*?"

"He *needs* you to do it. And he can't *ask* you. You have to offer, or it won't mean anything."

"What makes you think so?"

"He didn't come right out and tell me. But I know that's what he's thinking."

Aaron pondered a moment. "He asked once while I was there if I objected to him getting baptized. I just told him that was between him and the bishop."

Nick took Aaron's right hand in both of hers. "Aaron, he would like your forgiveness. If you could bring yourself to baptize him—you offer to do it—then it would be a sign that you had really forgiven him. He told me once that being baptized means nothing unless those he loves most— his family—can forgive him. He feels your mother, Regina, and your other two sisters have done that. He needs to know that you have."

Aaron turned his back to Nick and moved away a few steps, his mind racing back over the years, his heart re-experiencing the hurt. Then he recalled the more recent times in Preston that had gone a long way toward eliminating the remnants of his rage and resentment. Turning to face Nick, he asked, "Could I ask a favor?" As soon as the words were out, he remembered that evening when AJ had attempted to ask a favor of him.

"What's the favor?"

Aaron smiled thinly. "We're all beggars, aren't we? Sometimes we ask for a little. Sometimes a lot. But regardless of who we are, we have to beg."

"What are you talking about?"

"I was just thinking of AJ. He wanted to ask a favor of me. I figured he owed too much, that he didn't have the right to ask for any more. I suppose I owe a few debts too. Of course, I want someone to hear my requests and extend a little mercy. But I want to be stingy with everybody else. Especially AJ."

Aaron walked back to Nick and took her hand. "AJ doesn't have a phone. But if I call Bishop Tucker and he says we can baptize AJ this evening, will you go with me? AJ would want you there."

"Of course, I'll go. I'd go even if you didn't ask."

"Let's get you home, then," Aaron said, suddenly excited and anxious. "Then I'll go home and call and—"

"No," Nick broke in, shaking her head. "You go home and call. I'll run home and clean up and be waiting. We'll need to hurry."

They separated, Aaron going for his bike and Nick starting across the bridge. "Nick," Aaron called out suddenly. She stopped and turned. "If Bishop Tucker can't arrange it tonight, will you still go with me?"

"Where?"

"To Preston. We'll go to dinner at Juniper Upstairs. And then take the long ride home."

"Sure I will." She laughed. "Now move it, or we won't be going anyplace."

It was twenty minutes to nine. Aaron and Nick sat together on AJ's sofa, waiting for AJ to come out of his room. "You did say Regina, Brandon, and the kids are going to be there," AJ called out from his bedroom.

"They're already at the church."

"Do I need anything besides a towel? It's been a long time since I prepared for a baptism."

"You probably won't need a towel if you don't hurry,"

Aaron chided good naturedly. "Bishop Tucker will give up and go home."

"He did say nine o'clock, didn't he?"

"Yes, Mr. Tippets, he did say nine o'clock," Nick laughed. "Don't let Aaron rush you. You have plenty of time. And no one's going to do anything until you get there."

A moment later AJ came into the living room, dressed in a brown suit, white shirt, and tie. His gray hair was combed back and still wet. Under his arm he carried a flowered, yellow and white bath towel. "I guess I'm ready," he announced quietly. A grin broke his anxious features. "I feel like a kid again. Like I'm going to be all new after tonight."

Aaron pushed himself to his feet and pulled Nick up after him. "Let's go, so we can celebrate," Aaron said lightly.

"Eighteen years ago I was the one taking you. Now you're taking me."

Aaron nodded and Nick squeezed his arm as she pressed her lips together and struggled to hold back the threatening tears. AJ clenched the towel in his hands, wringing it nervously.

"Son, I would ask a favor of you before we go." He quickly held up a hand to ward off any protest. "I tried to ask once before," he went on quickly, "but you misunderstood. I wasn't going to ask you to take back my name." He shook his head sadly. "I forfeited that privilege years ago. But maybe what I ask will be harder for you to give. I'll understand if you can't."

He bowed his head and stared down at the wadded towel he clutched in his thin, rough, dark hands. "Son." He ran his tongue over his lips. "I would ask your forgiveness. I won't ask you to forget. There are too many tragic memories for that. If there is anything more that I need to do to heal the wounds, I'll do it. But, Son, I would like to go this evening with your forgiveness, if you can do that for an old man who was once your father."

Tears streamed down AJ's cheeks, and he couldn't bring himself to raise his gaze. If he had, he would have seen the tears in his son's eyes. Nick was crying also, and she brushed at her tears with her fingertips.

"I . . . " Aaron started hoarsely, his voice breaking. He swallowed back his flooding emotions. "I forgive you." His jaw clamped tight. "If you can forgive my hardened heart and stubborn ways." He hesitated and then burst out, "I love you, Dad."

At the mention of *dad*, AJ lifted his eyes as Aaron stepped forward and took him in his arms. And together they wept. Nick slipped silently from the house, sensing that this was a moment to be shared by only the father and the son.

It was past midnight when Nick and Aaron stood outside the Civic on the summit overlooking the black Bear Lake below them. They had stood there arm in arm for almost five minutes without speaking, just gazing out over the valley, with the moon shining and the stars blinking down from the night sky. There was a chill in the air, and Nick snuggled close to Aaron and leaned her head against his shoulder, so that he could cradle her in a comforting arm.

"Nick," Aaron said quietly, his lips brushing her hair, "I'm thinking of doing a couple of off-the-wall things."

"I'm in the mood for something radical."

"I've been thinking about it all day. I'm going to put off going back to law school. Maybe just for a year."

Nick straightened up and faced him. "So you won't go back to Tempe?"

He shook his head. "I'm going to try for that English job in Preston."

She smiled. "You're going to become a Jefferson High Indian?"

"I don't know how much longer AJ . . . I mean, Dad, is going to be around. I'd like to spend this next year close by."

Pushing up on her toes, she kissed him on the lips. "I wasn't sure what I was going to do when you left. It's a little late to transfer from USU to ASU. And I wasn't sure I had the personality to be a Sun Devil. What's the other off-the-wall thing?"

"I'd like you to marry me, Nick."

"That's off-the-wall?"

Aaron pulled her closer to him. "Maybe just the suddenness of the proposal."

"Suddenness?" Nick asked, laughing softly. "Actually, I've been wondering what has taken you so long. You know, if you had asked me a couple of weeks ago, we could have avoided a lot of—"

He squelched her sentence with a kiss.

"Do you care whether you're married to an English teacher or a lawyer?" he asked after a moment.

"Not as long as you can still be my coach."

"Is that a yes?"

She smiled up at him. "It's chilly. Hold me. And never let go. Ever."